THE KINGDOM OF STRANGERS

The *K*INGDOM *of* *S*TRANGERS

by *E*LIAS *K*HOURY

translated from the Arabic by
PAULA HAYDAR

THE UNIVERSITY OF ARKANSAS PRESS
Fayetteville 1996

Originally published in 1993
by Dār al-Ādāb in Beirut, Lebanon

Translation copyright 1996 by the
University of Arkansas Board of Trustees

Manufactured in the United States of America

oo   99   98   97   96   5   4   3   2   1

Designed by Alice Gail Carter

♾ The paper used in this publication
meets the minimum requirements of the American
National Standard for Permanence of Paper for
Printed Library Materials Z39.48-1984.

Library of Congress Cataloging-in-Publication Data
Khūrī, Ilyās.
    [Mamlakat al-ghurabā'. English]
    The kingdom of strangers / by Elias Khoury ;
translated from the Arabic by Paula Haydar.
        p.   cm.
    ISBN 1-55728-433-4 (alk. paper).—
ISBN 1-55728-434-2 (pbk. : alk. paper)
    I. Haydar, Paula, 1965–   . II. Title.
PJ7842.H823M3513   1996
892'.736—dc20   95-43341
                                    CIP

PREFACE

Elias Khoury was born in the Ashrafiyyeh district of Beirut, Lebanon, in 1948, a year which signals the beginning of one of the most troubling periods in the history of the Middle East, the end of which we are only now beginning to imagine both here in the West and in the Arab World as well. Having grown up in an atmosphere of discontent, struggle, and disenchantment, Khoury became an active participant in the Lebanese civil war, which began in 1975. He has lived through war—through all the chaos, violence, paranoia, tension, fear, and death—and has witnessed the disintegration of social order in Lebanon.

In a recent interview in the August 1993 edition of the Lebanese monthly literary magazine, *Al-Ādāb,* Elias Khoury discussed some of his concerns as a writer. He said:

> The truth is, what has terrified me most as long as I can remember is that I am a writer . . . the first thing I discovered is that we live in an oral society that doesn't write things down . . . My fear has been that our present and our past were subject to destruction.
>
> The other thing is that I am Lebanese . . . I discovered that this society had erased its history, as if it carried along with it a big fat eraser with which it blotted out its own history. So we have a situation where there is no written text about the war of 1860, and nothing about the revolution of 1920 or the revolution of 1958. What terrified me was that I was living a war (1975–) whose fate might well be similar to the fate of the wars that preceded it, and so I had to write it myself.

Here we have a declaration by a contemporary Lebanese writer that it is his purpose, his obsession, to record the "present." And, what a "present" indeed: civil war, faction-alism, violence, isolation, indifference, fear, death, change, instability, disbelief, doubt. These are the themes that impose themselves upon twentieth-century Lebanese writers. These are the conditions that pervade contemporary Lebanese society.

The Kingdom of Strangers (Mamlakat al-Gurabā) was pub-lished in Beirut in 1992 and is typical of Khoury's unique literary style. The Kingdom of Strangers is not a single story told in a linear time sequence; rather it is many stories and events told by a narrator who skips back and forth between past and present, between the literal and the highly poetic. Dialogue is often imbedded within the thoughts of the nar-rator. We, as readers, are allowed to enter the mind of the narrator and into his stream of consciousness. While reading, we begin to think like the narrator and see seemingly unre-lated things become connected the way only the human mind can connect them. As Elias Khoury said in the same inter-view in Al-Ādāb, "I write because I don't know, and my story unfolds in the process of writing. What is important is writing itself." Of all his novels The Kingdom of Strangers is the one in which Khoury best expresses his philosophy that stories are more important than the events themselves; the act of telling the story, or the fact there is a story to be told is more important than the truth of the details expressed by a particular narrator; moreover, truth is found in what people say because that is what people believe, even if they are lying. In The Kingdom of Strangers, Khoury chose to use the actual names of people, places and events, in order "to make it seem as though they were ficticious."

While all of his previous novels have centered around the

fragmentary world of war-torn Beirut, *The Kingdom of Strangers* also offers the western reader a first-hand look into the Israeli-Palestinian conflict. Khoury deals with the feelings of estrangement, suffering, loss, yearning, and anxiety felt by individuals on both sides of the struggle in his poignant, personal, and lyrical narrative. At a time when the prospects for resolution of the question of Palestine have come closer than ever before, a compassionate and intelligent view of the situation assumes great importance.

In addition to being a novel about Lebanon or Palestine, *The Kingdom of Strangers* is a bold and crafty work of literature. Writing less in the tradition of the modernists, such as Nobel laureate Naguib Mahfouz and more in the direction of postmodern Third-World writers such as Fuentes, Marquez, and Asturias, Elias Khoury brings into the development of the Arabic novel a new style and a new language. Its fragmentary nature presents a particular challenge to the translator and to the readers of the translation. The flashbacks and ratiocinations are presented in a variety of syntactic structures, ranging from simple declarative statements to extremely involved periodic sentences, which might create a sense of need for paragraph unity in a bewildered reader looking for logical connections and, therefore, tempt a helpful translator into the trap of interpretation. As translator, I have tried to reproduce Khoury's literary style, first, for its value as good literature and, second, to afford the English reader and writer a chance to appreciate and perhaps emulate the style of one of the Arab World's foremost novelists. Another important reason for translating this literary work is to respond to the following statement by Elias Khoury himself:

"My basic fear has always been that my works would be translated as social documents, as is the case for most examples of Arabic literature in translation, including those of Naguib Mahfouz. I am not interested in presenting a social document, because literature is only partially a social document. It is mostly literature!"

THE KINGDOM OF STRANGERS

told her I could smell the aroma of memories. She smiled.

Mary smiled whenever she didn't know what to say. Then she would mumble and hesitate before saying she didn't know how to express her thoughts.

That's how she was.

She had short hair and big, wide eyes. Her back was bent slightly forward, and she was singing a strange tune—she never did tell me where she got that tune—as she walked beside me along the shores of the Dead Sea.

The horizon was lead gray.

Lead colors the shores of the Dead Sea where I stand. The Jordan Valley sinks down with me into a damp abyss. Humidity, and lead, and the aroma of memories.

"The difference is the story," she said. "Love is the story of love."

She wasn't with me on my trip to the valley. Yes she was; the smell of her was there with me while I smelled memories, and she didn't know the difference between love and the story of love.

She said she loved me.

When I met her that night, she didn't mumble or hesitate. She kissed me and said she loved me and didn't ask about the difference between love and the story of love.

That's how things are in the beginning—as though they are suspended in midair.

I met her. It was night, and it was Beirut. We met on a balcony suspended above the sea. I had just come back from the Jordan Valley. My body was drenched with the smell of fatigue, and on my head was dust from the soil of Palestine. She was there. Some people I hardly knew came by, and we stayed up until three in the morning. They were dancing, and I felt alone, about to die. I was coming from death. That's what I said to her. She thought I was trying to flirt with her and laughed.

"Death," she said. "How nice!"

And she laughed.

I laughed, too, and we danced. She danced in front of me, her body held together by a thousand invisible threads. She was moving right and left in a single motion. I don't remember a lot. I don't know how to remember things. She was the one who told me. I took her to the sea. We went out in a sailboat, drifted from the shore out into the deep water. That was where she told me. Things looked to me like shadows, and it was as though we were shadows over words. I told her that what she said seemed reasonable. "I remember it because you're telling it to me." She laughed. I haven't forgotten that laugh. How can I forget? She was dancing, and I was dancing; then she went to sleep. She didn't sleep. She went to the balcony and lay down on a hammock. I walked toward her. Her eyes were closed, but she saw me. She saw me with her eyes without opening her eyes. She saw me coming, and so she moved over a little as if to leave me a small space to lie down next to her. I held onto the edge of the hammock and then gave it a push. There was the wind of September. That year it rained in September. It always rains

—4—

in September. Beirut in September seems wet with the beginnings of winter. Winter adorns the hem of its skirt, as though it were the hem of a woman's skirt. September is always like that—like a woman running, her dress getting soaked in the rain. I couldn't see the woman's face. I was looking at her from behind. Her dress was long, embroidered with red designs, and she was running, with water dripping from the bottom of her dress. Mary was sleeping as I held onto the rope of the hammock, and the air, moist with the smell of water, covered her face.

Her face was covered with water, with what looked like water. Then I went closer and lay down beside her. She didn't say a word. I shut my eyes the way she had shut hers, and I saw her the way she had seen me, and the hammock cradled us like a ship rocking in the middle of a calm sea.

She said she opened her eyes and found that everyone had gone.

She woke me up and asked me that question she had asked me a thousand times. She opened her eyes and said something like "Welcome." Then she asked me who I was. She didn't know my name. I hadn't told her. She knew my name after that, but never used it when she talked to me. She opened her eyes and asked me who I was, and so I laughed, and hugged her close to my chest, and left her embedded there inside me.

That night, which I remember because she told it to me, or I told it to her, I don't know which, and I don't know why lovers never stop telling their stories, which they already know. With her I learned that stories are told because they are known, and that, when they tell their stories to each other, people transform the past into the present. Stories exist solely for the purpose of making the past present.

She asked me who I was and got up, so I followed her. We went into the living room. There was a mattress on the floor. She said to come over, and I went. I lay down next to her and made love to her. I don't remember her getting undressed, but I do remember her being naked next to me on the mattress on the living room floor. I remember that whiteness that was like the froth of a crashing wave, and I remember the ship.

A few years later she asked me if I would call the night of the hammock and the mattress "sex."

I laughed.

It wasn't sex, and it wasn't love. I didn't take her the way you take a woman. I used to think a woman is taken from the outside in, and when you make love to a woman, you enter her. But with her, it wasn't . . . we were together; I entered her, and I didn't enter her. It was as though I didn't enter her. I was beside her and with her and in her. Sex came like flowing water, as if it were an extension of my body and hers, as if without any entrance or exit, like a dream, like the dreams we don't remember but that leave traces on our eyes. That's how I was. As though I were in a boat, rocking, as though I were in the sea, watching a seagull skim over the water and the water doesn't cover him. As though I were the water. Water doesn't cover itself; water is covered and covers others. I was covered, and I was covering her. I was, I don't know what, but I remember we were laughing. Five hours of nonstop laughter. We were laughing as though we had discovered laughter, as though we had discovered the way things resonate as they emerge from the throat, and lips, and eyes.

That day she said she loved me, and laughed.

We didn't laugh because we didn't believe. We laughed

because we did believe. Believing in things is like not believing; it leads to laughter. "For five hours you've been flying over me. I greet you, and then I send you off, laughing."

That's what she said.

That's how she always told the story.

"And tomorrow when the story ends, we'll sit on the shore, get drunk, laugh, and then go our separate ways. I don't want any sad endings."

She talked about the end of love before it had even started. She talked about love as though it were a story she already knew from beginning to end.

"Stories don't end," I said to her.

"What does end?" she asked.

"The storyteller ends," I answered.

"You are the storyteller," she said.

"No. I am the story."

She laughed. "That's just like you."

"That's how I am," I said. I told her all about the Dead Sea—the sea of salt, the sea of water, the sea of the dividing line between earth and sky.

I told her all the stories, and I asked her to come with me. She said she hadn't found a place. The boat had set out, and she too must set out to wherever it was she was going.

She asked me how love ends, and left.

And today I see her.

I see her in front of me like a woman drenched by the rain. I see her from behind as she walks quickly through the streets of Beirut smudged by the September rain. I see her, and I tell her I see her, and I let her go I don't know where.

"I don't like balconies," she said.

She said the sea makes her feel dizzy.

She said she loved me.

She said she was the story.

Her name is Mary. I forgot to tell you that her name is Mary, that she has white skin like Widad, that she has a body that becomes colored with desire when desire takes hold of it. And that she is now—I don't know.

I took her to the Dead Sea. I remember taking her. We walked before the lead gray horizon. She cried when she saw the lights of Jerusalem sneaking out from behind the city of Jericho. She ran out into the salty sea and said she was walking on water. She drank a bottle of white wine and told me endless stories about men and women she had known and loved.

All the stories I know and don't know came together there on that bank chipped out of that salty, gray sea. A gray sea that doesn't look like other seas, and behind us cities that slide down into the Jordan Valley as though being swallowed, one by one, down into the earth, down to a place that cannot be reached, to stories that go on and on, that seem to have no end.

And the story goes on.

When I returned this time around, with memories covering me rather than dust, and the taste of my desire for life now dry and bitter, I told her the story of the monk who died, and I tried to play with her the game of telling the stories we know.

"I wasn't with you," she said.

"Love is the story of love," I said.

"And when does love end?" she asked.

"When the story ends," I answered.

"And when does the story end?"

"When the storyteller dies."

— 8 —

"And when does the storyteller die?"

"Here you have to change the question. You have to ask, 'Who killed the storyteller?'"

"And who killed the storyteller?" she asked.

"I don't know."   ♦

What am I writing about?

Two stories. No, three. I don't know how many stories, and I don't know why they become linked together when I tell them. When we write we have the power to say whatever we want. No, we have the power to say what has been said. We want what we say. Not the opposite.

But why?

Why does the image of white Widad appear, over the face of Jesus, with the Jordan river, with the Marys surrounding the man on His way to His death? Is it that memories, when recalled, get jumbled together and form into a mixture, into a single story with its roots in all the stories?

But they are not my memories.

Do I dare say, Master, that Your story is my memories? Do I dare expect You to answer?

I told Samia they weren't my memories as we stood in Shatila Refugee Camp, in front of the demolished mosque which had been turned into a graveyard. I did not even say the word "love." Her name was Samia. No, Mary. Samia comes to this vast field of stories and enters into them, and says she is Mary. The truth is, I told her we would change the world. I spoke to her about changing the world not knowing what I was saying. I said we would change the world, because that's what we used to say.

On the shores of the lead gray sea she asked me about the world.

"Has the world changed?" she asked.

This time she didn't hesitate when she asked, and she didn't swallow half of her words as she always did. I was the one who hesitated, for I hadn't changed the world. But I had discovered the most basic thing, the most commonplace and naive thing. I discovered that I was going to die, because men die. When I discovered the world, death changed, or vice versa—when I discovered death, the world changed. I didn't change it. I saw it. And when I saw, everything changed— I and he and you and she.

Perhaps, for this reason, the stories blend together and transform themselves into this story. Thus the story, as Mary does not know, begins when it is no longer a story, and mixes with other stories, and there the love doesn't die even after the hero dies.

White Widad, the Circassian woman, didn't know, as she settled in Beirut after a long journey of wandering and degradation, that she would end up in this killing field and would become the ground that this story covers, in order to create stories about this strange world that we haven't changed.

Why am I telling this?

Is it to tell Mary I love her, even though I've told her a thousand times? Words no longer mean anything, for she isn't here, and she won't read what I'm writing. Even if she did read it, she wouldn't know I love her. Or do we write because we are not heroes?

Heroes die. We, on the other hand, tell their stories.

So let me define things. I am talking about one woman named Mary. This woman is the one who took me to the green line in Beirut where I saw all the destruction we caused. Then I went up with her to a demolished restaurant that used to be called "Lucolus," located on the top floor of a tall building overlooking the sea. Mary carried the pot of beans and rice she had prepared at her house, and we climbed the broken stairs and the dilapidated building until we reached the place where the restaurant had been. We sat on the floor because there weren't any chairs. We ate, and we drank arak, and she told me everything.

Samia is another story altogether.

When I held Samia by the hand, in front of Ali Abu Tawq's grave inside Shatila Refugee Camp, I called her Mary, and so she bowed her head as if she really were Mary.

Here lies the fundamental flaw.

Heroes bow their heads when we tell their stories. Even Fawzi al-Qawuqji bowed his head as he listened to an account of his memoirs.

The general commander of the Rescue Army was seventy years old when we met him at the Palestine Research Center in Beirut. He was standing in the office of the center director, Dr. Anise Sayyigh, recounting his memories of his army's heroic deeds. Then he put his right leg up on the chair and rolled up the bottom of his pants to show us the scars.

"Nine bullets," he said.

Fawzi al-Qawuqji was tall and slender. He paid no attention to his white, full-figured German wife, who was standing next to him, trying to push the leg of his pants back down over his leg.

Heroes pay no attention.

The hair on al-Qawuqji's long, white leg had long since fallen out, leaving behind nothing but dark grooves all over his leg. He paid no attention to his German wife as she tried to push his pant leg down.

Heroes tell stories only when they become heroes.

But do heroes know they're going to become heroes? Did Ali know, as he ran beneath the bombs, through the besieged alleys of Shatila, that he would become a hero, and his story would become a story?

Fawzi al-Qawuqji believed the story.

He was standing in the middle of the room. We were all around him as he narrated. We had already read his book of memoirs, and even though he told some of those same stories, we listened to him as though we'd never read them. He told us how the armies joined forces in the Jordan Valley, about the various cavalry units that met there and how they crossed the river to Palestine. But he wasn't telling the truth. The cavalry units he told us about had actually met in the valley in 1936, not 1948. In 1936, al-Qawuqji was leading a group of volunteers. In 1948, he was in command of an army. But when he stood before us to tell the story, he didn't distinguish between the two wars. He talked about himself as though he had been born the commander of the Rescue Army, and we listened to him and believed him. Why not believe him? What's the difference between 1936 and 1948? Or tomorrow, when I stand there, or Ali stands? But Ali will not stand, because he died. But let's suppose Ali didn't die. Ali deserves to stand more than I do because he's like al-Qawuqji. He took five bullets to the leg. When I met him for the first time his left leg was in a cast. He limped, leaning on a cane. After his leg healed and he didn't limp anymore, he still carried the cane. Whenever he became self-conscious he would limp a little, as though he'd grown accustomed to limping and no longer wanted to walk the way he did before his left leg was shot as he fought at the entrance to Birjawi Quarter in Beirut.

Let's suppose Ali were telling the story.

Let's suppose I'm standing, with a group of people around me, in the very same Palestine Research Center, which was turned into a graveyard after the Israeli invasion of 1982 when they blew it up with a car bomb. Hanni Shaheen, who had come from Fasoota in Galilee, was killed; Suad was paralyzed; and thirty employees ended up in the hospital. The mangled bodies remained on Columbani Street for three days before the sanitation workers came and sprayed the quarter with water and disinfectants.

Let's suppose everything went back to the way it was, and Ali is standing there reciting his memoirs for us, old age having left its white mark on his head.

What would he tell?

Would he find enough space in his memory to differentiate between the battle of September 1970 in Jordan and the 1985 siege of Shatila Refugee Camp in Beirut?

Or would he forget a little and tell us about Samia, as if she had been his comrade at the Freedom Fighter Base in Ghawr al-Safi, and about his children who are studying in Amman even though they were going to study in Tunis?

I see him before me just as I saw al-Qawuqji.

Al-Qawuqji was tall and slim. Ali, on the other hand, was short and skinny and had a heavy beard and eyebrows so thick they formed a straight line across his forehead. I can see him, reciting his heroic deeds, forgetting the actual dates.

"Why do you all believe?" Mary asked.

"I don't know," I answered. "We believe because we feel defeat. The victor is concerned with the truth. He separates time into stages, distinguishing between one stage and the next, because he wants to control the past and the future. As for us?"

"What about us?" she asked.

"We haven't been defeated yet," I said.

"And what do you call what's going on?"

"One defeat after another. But I can't believe it."

"You don't believe it because you are defeated. You believe your own stories, and you forget the truth." ♦

And Mary knew.

She told me she knew that young man was going to look at her, and his eyes would fill up with desire. I forgot to tell you that when we went up to the demolished restaurant, the war had ended, and the Lebanese Army had been deployed in downtown Beirut. Mary and I went to Lucolus Restaurant, and we saw the weary soldiers sitting on the ground outside the building amid the rubble and the destruction. They were from the Aghrar Platoon of the Lebanese Army— new recruits in their first three to six months of service. We asked the group of young men, who were lighting a fire next to the building, where they were from. They said they were from the north. We invited them to eat lunch with us, but they were reluctant. There were five soldiers; three came up with us; two stayed below. The tall, dark young man with the thin, black mustache was looking at Mary, and she was smiling back at him. Then he started telling her stories about his family. I didn't listen. Mary's ability to listen and encourage the others to talk surprised me. Then she disappeared. She went with the tall, dark soldier to serve some food to the other soldiers keeping guard downstairs, and she didn't come back for a long time. ♦

Time is long.

That's how I felt when I sank in the sea, that time is long. I knew I wouldn't become a hero. I attempted heroism

— 14 —

once and failed. I got out of the fishing boat—when we were fishing in the sea, at Ayn al-Mraysi. I got out and walked on the water. I told them I would walk on water, and I did. They all saw me walk. That's what they told me, but I saw myself sink. I was sinking, the water spreading over me like a blanket. Peter the Apostle was afraid when he sank. He sank because he was afraid, and so Jesus woke up and rescued him. As for me, no one came to save me. I didn't want anyone. I wanted to walk and to sink. I sank and didn't walk. They all said they saw me walk, but actually I sank. Then I believed what the others said. This is heroism—believing what others tell you.

Mary believed she went with that tall, dark soldier. I told her that, and she believed it. This is what made her something worth writing about.

She told me how she felt sorry for the young man. She let him kiss her hand, and then she saw him die.

"He kissed my hand and walked away," she said.

"I saw him walking in the middle of the street. He was waving to me to follow him. I wanted to follow him, but I couldn't move. And then I heard the explosion."

Mary saw the young soldier die when a mine exploded in the middle of the street. She didn't go near him; she was afraid of his mangled body parts that had been splattered all over the walls.

This is what heroism is all about.

To believe what others tell about you. Then you become their stories, and you die.

The only flaw in my story is that I didn't die, and neither did Fawzi al-Qawuqji when he lifted up his right leg, put it on the chair, and told us how his son was killed in Germany. But he believed. As for me, no. Believe, no.

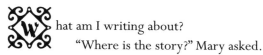hat am I writing about?

"Where is the story?" Mary asked.

I told her I was telling Samia's story, not hers. And I know that what I've told so far does not work even as an introduction to the story of the Dead Sea, or the story of Widad, or of Emil.

But I'm not writing a story.

I just let things come to me. I say I'm telling the story as it is, and I wanted to say also "nothing added, nothing removed," but I changed my mind. And so, Widad the Circassian, who's been dead for ten years now, resembles this broken mannequin I can see now on the balcony of George Naffaa's Commissions Office. Poor George Naffaa. I say "poor" because he died. I grieve over him, and it has nothing to do with the poet Fuad Gabriel Naffaa, who also died, but remains in my memory as though he were a statue. He would walk along the streets of Ashrafiyyeh (also called "Little Mountain") hovering around Julia's house near the headquarters of the Red Cross, some wrinkled papers in his jacket pockets—his new collection of poetry. He smoked Bafras and never said hello to anyone. Poor Fuad Gabriel Naffaa. He died, too. This is how the living absolve themselves of having betrayed the dead, with a few sympathetic words about them that have absolutely no meaning. We

betray the dead, constantly. Writing about them is the ultimate betrayal of the dead. No, this is not correct. The very
fact that we continue to live, in spite of all this death, is the
ultimate betrayal. And so we take refuge in memories to
avoid being disloyal, but in the end, what do we remember?
Nothing but ourselves.

Samia was the only one who, when she told me about
Ali's death, did not talk about herself. Usually people tell you
about other people's deaths so they can talk about their own
sorrow and pain. When Samia told me about Ali's death, she
talked about his body having been torn apart by shrapnel and
how the doctor locked the door to the room where he was
trying treat him, even though he knew he was dead.

Her black eyes didn't shed a single tear. But as we stood
holding hands in front of the demolished mosque that had
been turned into a graveyard, there was a kind of fog around
her eyes.

The doctor who treated the already-dead Ali was a Greek
called Dr. Yanu. He tried to bring Ali back to life before
finally coming out of the room in tears. Dr. Yanu had worked
with the Palestinian Red Crescent in Cairo ten years earlier
while he completed his studies. He was a Greek, whose
family had immigrated to Canada, studying in Cairo. After
that, he would become the only doctor in Shatila Refugee
Camp, which was held under siege for three long years. That
is a story worth telling. Dr. Yanu wrote a book about the
siege and the death of Ali. He told me how they brought Ali
to him, dead.

"I took him. . . ," he said. "I took him in my arms and
brought him to the operating room. I laid him on the ground
and locked the door with the key. I knew he was dead, but I
couldn't believe it. The way his body continued to shudder

gave the impression that there was something going on beyond the realm of medicine and science. I saw his soul. It was his soul that shuddered for half an hour or more as it withdrew with savage brutality from his dead body, as if it didn't want to leave, as if it had been surprised by death and wanted to reject death. The body was dead. I knew that even before I touched him. They carried him, and his body shuddered like a slaughtered animal's. His chest was split open, and he was dead. I took him into my arms the way I would hold a baby. Ali had become a baby again. Suddenly, the tension lifted from his face, and he became tender. He trembled like an infant seconds after his mother has given birth to him. I put him down on the floor and told everyone to leave. I sent them out and locked the door with the key. I didn't do anything. I ripped open his shirt and saw the wounds and the shrapnel and the blood that had ceased to flow as though something had blocked it—like a dam. His blood was like water, but it had coagulated. I looked at his half-closed eyes and shut them with my fingers. His eyes were tender, like two wilted roses. I learned about death from eyes. Eyes wilt all of a sudden, just as flowers do. The eye is the flower of the body, the refuge of the soul. His soul had lost its refuge and begun searching for a place to go. The body was trembling, and I, the doctor who had saved the lives of hundreds of wounded men and women, found myself incapable of saving his. That man was my closest friend. In that camp surrounded by destruction and fear, I was alone. I was alone, and if it hadn't been for him, I'd have died of loneliness. I can see him now, dying right before my eyes. He died before I did, and I didn't do anything. Suddenly I shed that part of me that was a doctor. Never in my life had I felt like a magician except in that siege. There I felt more like a demigod. I saved people with miracles alone. Do you know what it means to be a doctor under such conditions? No one knows—not enough antibiotics, not enough anesthesia, not enough nurses, not even enough diesel to run the generator. Not enough of anything, and yet I would work miracles. The day Ali died, the miracles stopped working. I saw death and felt completely powerless. I watched his soul as it tried to ward off the death that had taken hold of his eyes. I saw his soul and sat down on the ground next to his body. I wanted to massage his shaking body and help the soul to leave. But I didn't dare. I was afraid. I sat beside him and was afraid. When his body relaxed, I felt I was going to faint, that I needed to sleep. I almost did fall asleep. I heard her knocking at the door. When I opened it, she said she'd been knocking for half an hour, but I hadn't heard her. She didn't ask me about him. She didn't ask. Samia knew. She came close to him and cast a glance over him as though to cover him. She took me by my hand and told me I was exhausted and should go and get some rest. I went out of the room and left her with him. I heard her shut the door behind me. But I didn't ask her anything. I slept for ten hours straight, and I didn't ask her. I slept like the dead. I didn't hear the bombs, and I didn't dream of anything."

The Greek doctor shows me around the hospital. I see half-demolished rooms and open curtains that seem to be suspended in midair. I walk beside him as he shows me the medical supply room. I can smell the medicine, and then I ask about the operating room, and the doctor smiles.

Samia didn't speak. She was watching us. She listened to him explain how Ali died, and she didn't say anything. She smiled as she drank her coffee, her hands wrapped around the cup, trying to warm them. I could see the semblance of a smile on her lips.

That smile has flashed in my memory time and time again.

The Greek doctor left, of course, went to Canada or some other country; I don't know where. And Ali stayed just where he was, with his body shuddering, his soul hovering over head, and the sounds of thousands of bombs filling the sky.

As for George Naffaa's balcony, it seemed as if it were hanging, alone, in midair.

Dust, and that destruction enveloping downtown Beirut, people walking among the debris as if searching for their lost city, or discovering it. Out on the balcony, around the side of the building, the mannequin stood out—the mannequin of a naked woman with pink skin and blonde hair. The left hand was broken, the right extended, and the head was twisted around backward amidst torn cardboard boxes and broken furniture. It seems whoever broke into the apartment put her out there to get rid of her.

"She's Circassian. Look," Mary said.

The mannequin was Circassian. That's how people saw Circassian women—with blonde hair and white skin—pinkish skin.

We were going down the hill from the Church of the Capuchins toward Patriarch Huwayyek Street, searching for Lucolus Restaurant, when we saw the Circassian mannequin on George Naffaa's balcony.

"She's white Widad," Mary said

We walked toward Huwayyek Street.

"This is where Khalil died," I said to her.

"Don't you remember?" she said. "You've told me that a thousand times."

What am I writing?

"Where's the flaw?" I asked her.

"Never mind," she said.

And the mannequin came down. Mary was trying to run toward the street when she saw the mannequin. It wasn't a mannequin. It was a woman—a seventy-year-old woman, white as white can be. They used to call her the "white lady." That's what George Naffaa used to call his father's wife. He said she was the white lady. He said his father converted to Islam in order to marry her. At first no one took the story seriously. Iskandar Naffaa and the Jew Wadee al-Sukhun were business partners. They owned the well-known commissions office near Librairie Antoine, behind Riyad al-Suluh Square.

And they brought her.

She was a young girl, not more than thirteen years old. She was trembling, afraid, didn't speak any Arabic. And he bought her. In those days, a group of merchants and highway robbers worked between Beirut, Alexandria, and Russia. They would kidnap young girls, or buy them, and sell them in the white slave markets of Cairo, Damascus, and Beirut. That was in 1920, the year the state of Greater Lebanon was declared, and when Beirut was recovering from the effects of World War I and memories of the famine from which George Naffaa's family would not have been spared had it not been for the protection of Naseem al-Sukhun, Wadee's father and Iskandar's partner, who managed to smuggle wheat from Hauran and sell it to wealthy families in Beirut.

Iskandar Naffaa, who was in his fifties, brought home the trembling young girl he had bought. He didn't tell his wife, Madame Lody, that he had bought her. He told her she was a maid. And so the maid entered the house, and the story began.   ◆

I don't know why I thought of Wadee al-Sukhun when I met Emil Azayev. Emil was the first Israeli I'd ever met.

New York, 1981.

The civil war in Lebanon had transformed into *White Faces,* and I was in New York doing a study on Palestinian folklore. I was researching the character Jurji the monk.

At the Columbia University library I met Emil. He had a thick beard and a dark complexion and spoke American English with a Middle Eastern accent. He'd stretch out his letters with a kind of drawl which made his words seem wide, as though they occupied a vast expanse, unlike Americans, who clutch onto their words and then let them fly out of their mouths.

Emil Azayev introduced himself as an Israeli student living in New York. He invited me to see a short film produced by a friend of his about "Canada Park" in Jerusalem. That is, about the three villages—Amwas, Bayt Nuba, and Yalu—which the Israelis destroyed immediately after occupying the West Bank in 1967, and where they created Canada Park in order to extend the city limits of Jerusalem.

On the shores of the Dead Sea, I saw my friend Emil.

We were sitting in the Jordan Valley, beneath a lead gray sky.

The return to Amman is the return to a city whose memory never runs dry. Perhaps this is because when we went there the first time we were filled with that yearning for newness that dies as you grow older.

From Amman we went to the valley, to the Jordan River, where our baptism with water, with the Holy Spirit, and with blood began.

And in front of the river I met him.

Jesus was everywhere. He was standing in the middle of the shallow waters—the Israelis had diverted the tributaries, causing the river to become nothing but a little muddy stream. There at the little muddy stream I saw Him. Jesus was standing, all alone, like a stranger. And I was right in front of Him. That day they asked Him, just as they will ask Him every day, "Are you Elias?" And He will answer them as He always did, "No."

This time they asked me. I don't know where they came from, or why. I saw them there, suddenly, before me, and they asked me, "Are you Elias?"

I said, "No."

They said, "Then who?"

I said, "Me."

They said, "Who?"

I said, "Just the one writing this story."

Jesus turned to look. The water was up to His knees, and He was standing as though listening to mysterious voices we couldn't hear.

He turned and asked me, "What story?"

"Your story, Master," I said.

"But it is written," He said.

"I am writing it because it is written," I said. "We always write what has been written. If it were not written, we would not write it."

And a man over there asked Him, "Are you the Messiah?"

"It is as you say," He answered. He didn't say He was. He let them say it. He said only what had already been said before.

In this way, Master, I write what is already written. Otherwise, what would I write?

The horizon was lead gray, and He was there—He, and Elias the prophet of fire, and that short distance separating land from land.

Emil was not with me.

I had listened to his story in New York, and he had really loved the character of the monk. He said he was worthy of having an entire novel written about him—an Arab folk hero, like Robin Hood. But Emil thought the monk might be accused of being antisemitic. He suggested changing the part where he kidnaps the Jew.

I told Emil that the monk did not kidnap any Jews, that folk tales say things so they won't happen; they are a kind of psychological compensation. Emil insisted he was right and was not convinced that it was at all possible for us to write the story.

But there's a big difference. I mean, between Emil's story and Wadee al-Sukhun's, because Wadee al-Sukhun did not have a story. His story is that he didn't have a story, and so he felt compelled to adopt one, in order to immigrate to Israel after the short civil war that took place in Lebanon in 1958. At that time, he sold everything, and the buyer was George Naffaa.   ◆

Emil told the story.

He told how his father, Albert, fled Poland and went to Palestine.

Albert Azayev was walking along one of the streets of Sofia when he saw the truck taking Jewish prisoners to the death camps. He saw his only brother aboard the truck. He could see his head through the barbed wire. Albert saw his brother and clung to the wall. He had searched for a place to hide, but found only the wall. He clung to it, trembling with fear. Just then the brother started to scream. Albert said he saw his brother shouting and jumping and gesturing with his head toward him. Albert nearly fell to his knees from the bone-breaking fear. Was the prisoner trying to tell his captors to take Albert, too? Did he want to tell them that this man clinging to the wall was another Jew and should be taken prisoner? Or was he afraid for Albert and wanted to warn him?

Albert never knew.

He told the story to his son only once, and in Emil's mind, the matter remained forever ambiguous. When his father told him the story, he was all choked up, and his voice was filled with terror.

"Did my brother want me killed? Or was he acting out of fear? Fear can make people do just about anything."

And so, Albert Azayev arrived in Palestine by way of the Jewish Agency. He had wanted to go to Switzerland to attend the School of Hotel Management in Lausanne, but instead he wound up in Tel Aviv. Tel Aviv was supposed to be just a stop on his way to Lausanne, but then he met his wife, a young woman of Russian origin, who was born in Palestine, and he stayed there with her.

"My father didn't want to return to Palestine," Emil said.

"You mean go," I said.

"He didn't want to return," he said.

"You mean go," I said.

Albert Azayev was not like Faysal.

How can I write Faysal's story when Faysal died before his story ended? Was he the same young man I met after the 1982 massacres of Sabra and Shatila? I don't know.

I asked Muhammad Malas, the Syrian film producer, but when he came with me to Shatila to visit Samia, Faysal had already been killed. He had been shot in the head three days before Ali Abu Tawq was killed.

Muhammad Malas, who had made a film about the dreams of Palestinians, didn't include Faysal in his film. Instead he published the full text of Faysal's dream in a book.

Faysal said:

"It was just like the stories our parents used to tell us, how they left Palestine in '48. Exactly like that. I dreamed that all of us from the camp were on trucks, with all our belongings, except now we were returning to Palestine. After we crossed al-Naqura, I saw a big lake. I looked and asked my dad what it was. He said, 'What's the matter, Son; don't you know? That's Lake Tiberias.' At that moment my dad's words filled me with joy, and I started looking all around. From the moving truck, I could see the land; everything was green—so green—there were olive trees everywhere. And only in the dream did we arrive in Palestine. Suddenly everyone from the camp headed off in different directions, each to his own village. Those from Haifa went to Haifa, those from Yaffa went to Yaffa. And I found myself all alone. All my school friends had gone. I felt so lonely and started saying to myself, 'If only we could go back, all of us from the refugee camp, go back and make a little town. A town, or a village, or a camp, something like Shatila, where we were before.' I went to look for my friends right away, to tell them, 'Come, let's build a little town, a town or a village or a camp, something like Shatila, where we were before.' I went to look for my friends right away to tell them, 'Come, let's build a town in the heart of Palestine that can bring us together and be like the camp.' And then I woke up."

Faysal woke up. He was eleven years old. He woke up because he knew he would never return to Palestine—he would go there. No one will return. Return is a fantasy. We return—that is to say, we go.

Why go if we can't return?

"Did the Jews return?" I asked Emil.

Faysal came back another time to tell another story. His second story wasn't a dream: it was what happened. The dream happened, and the massacre happened.

They were piled on top of each other. Faysal had been shot three times, in the waist and the hand. He crawled over and lay down between his seven brothers and sisters and his mother, who had all been killed by the bullets of those who entered Shatila Refugee Camp the night of September 16, 1982. He hid among the dead to make it look as though he were dead, but he wasn't. When the armed men left, he ran into the street. Then he crawled between the corpses— those black, bloated corpses, surprised by death, as Jean Genet described them—until he got to where the foreign reporters were stationed, and there he passed out.

Faysal did not tell his third story, because the third time he died.

Emil said this tragedy must end.

I was standing along the waist of the Dead Sea.

The Dead Sea looks like the waist of the world. That's what Mahmoud Darwish would have said if he had come there with me. He would have said he would run right over there and return. He would enter Jericho, and climb the hills of Jerusalem. The lights of Jerusalem peer through the gray color that separates the Jordan Valley from the land above.

"Will you return?" I would ask.

And he would answer with another question, "Whoever said land is inherited like language?"

And I would tell him the story of Jerusalem. I would tell

him that the Arab Sufis believed Jerusalem was located at that point nearest to both Heaven and Hell. On its hills you can listen to the hymns of Heaven and smell the fragrance of Heaven, and in its valleys, you can hear the cries of Hell and smell the odor of Hell. For this reason the Sufis refused to live there, and advised people to leave it because it is the city of lamentation. He would shake his head as he listened to the story, hiding his surprise behind his thick glasses, and he would talk to me about "Truce with the Mongols," a poem he recently published.

"Truce with the Mongols is impossible," I would say to him, "because truce presupposes coming to terms with the truth."

"What is truth?" Mary asked me.

"It is the meeting of two lies." Is it possible for two lies to meet above one land and give it its truth?

"Which two lies?" Mary asked.

"Emil and the monk," I answered.

"And Faysal?"

"Not Faysal. He is the dream. He is the story I'm trying to tell."

"But you're telling a different story."

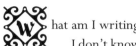hat am I writing?

I don't know. I feel the words coming loose, falling apart.

We are in front of the Dead Sea.

"It is the Sea of Salt. It's called the Sea of Araba, the Eastern Sea, the Sea of Sodom. The Sea of Salt is sixteen miles east of Jerusalem and can be seen clearly from the Mount of Olives. It is in the deepest part of the valley stretching from the Gulf of Aqaba to al-Hula. It is forty-six miles long, with a maximum width of ten and a half miles. It has an area of approximately three hundred square miles. Its waters are clear and contain 25 percent salts, half of which are ordinary salt, and half, others, including magnesium chloride, which gives it its bitter flavor. Ezekiel mentions that the restoration of the Dead Sea and the proliferation of many kinds of fish in it will be among the signs of life in God's New Kingdom."

"Is this where Jesus walked?" Mary asked.

"No," I said. "He walked on Lake Tiberias, which was called the Sea of Galilee."

"And here?"

"Here, no one."

But I see Him today, that is, in 1991, at the end of this gruesome century which began with a massacre and ended with a crime. I see Him, alone, dead, hanging on the cross, walking on the water.

He is the only real stranger.

A stranger in the kingdom of strangers He tried to establish. That's what the white Circassian believed.

Once a year, on Good Friday, she would go to the Church of the Virgin Mary. In the Holy Funeral Procession, she would always find a place for herself to the right of the iconostasis, next to the Bishop's seat, and chant all of the prayers. When the cantor would reach the hymn of "The Stranger," she would kneel down with the others and sing in a loud voice as the coffin circled over the heads of the worshipers. Everyone watched the coffin, waiting to be blessed by it, everyone but her, for she would be carried away with the hymn of the stranger, her voice raised in song. The cantor Elias Mitri, who was known for his strict adherence to Byzantine chanting, would pause from his own chanting from time to time in order to give her voice prominence and allow everyone to hear her.

Give me this stranger,
Who from his youth has wandered like a stranger,
Give me this stranger,
Whom his kinsmen killed in hatred like a stranger,
Give me . . .

She would sing, tears in her eyes, her slight, feminine voice intermingling with Elias Mitri's strong voice, while the people cried, the coffin circled, and death circled.   ♦

Iskandar Naffaa would look at this stranger who had entered his life as though he were swallowing her with his eyes. He wished he could become an extension of her strange, white body. True, he never had any children by her, but he was in love with her his whole life. Old age came early for Iskandar Naffaa. When he married Widad the Circassian, he was fifty years old. She was fourteen. Three years after their marriage, he started getting sick. He had a heart attack, and many other health problems followed. At first, none of his five children visited him. Lody, his first wife, ordered them not to see him and to let him die like a dog. Then, as time passed, and because Naffaa's old age stretched on endlessly, his children started visiting him again. Then they got reintroduced to the "Circassian bitch," as their mother called her. They saw how she took care of him, pulling him out from the jaws of death, as though in her hands she held the secret of his life, as though her magic and her beauty were the fine thread holding him onto life.

"If it weren't for her, my father would have died," George said to his mother.

"To Hell with him," Madame Lody screamed and then started to cry.

At her children's insistence she went to see him. There she saw the white Circassian. She no longer looked like a maid. She had become a lady. Lody entered the house, shuddering with hatred. When the Circassian saw her, she rushed toward her, kissed her hand, and cried. And George Naffaa watched that white beauty of hers as it turned into a story.

I told Mary about Widad the Circassian.

I told her how she left the house, alone. She had suffered through some difficult days. She turned down her husband's son's offer to go and stay at his house. She was all alone beneath the bombing and the fear, in her small house in which she had lived for thirty years taking care of sick Iskandar, and then thirty years more without visiting anyone or receiving any visitors. She went to church every Sunday morning, worked as a volunteer in the nursing home, and loved everyone. When she got sick, she refused to leave her house. She told George to go take care of his family and then shut her eyes. The son could hear her humming the two lines of poetry she had recited to his father the moment of his death.

Iskandar was nearly unconscious, Widad beside him, holding his hand, and George, Katia, Ruba, Samar, and Jacqueline all in the room. He opens his eyes for a moment. His daughter Katia rushes to his side. He looks over at Widad, who is leaning over him by his head, reciting the poetry of Imru al-Qays, whom he loved. Iskandar smiles, then closes his eyes.

"He died smiling," George said.

And now Widad lay in her bed, refusing to leave her home. The son leaned over her, and so she recited the two lines and smiled, but she didn't die as her husband had died thirty years before.

> O neighbor mine, the time of visiting draws near
> And I will remain forever with you here
> O neighbor mine, here are we, two strangers
> And every stranger, to a stranger, is dear

She recited the lines, but she didn't die.

A few days later, she went out into the street.

No, no, before she went out, that strange thing happened.

The end was stranger than the beginning.

I said to Mary that the end can be stranger. This is Beirut, and Beirut turns things into a breath of familiar strangeness. They tell you their stories, and you feel that you have heard them before, and yet you are surprised. Beirut is like that, surprise at strange things that give you an obscure feeling of familiarity.

"We don't know the beginning," Mary said. "We think we know it, but we don't know anything." She said we don't even know the beginning of Widad the Circassian. We don't, and neither does Widad. She herself has forgotten. What should we expect from a young girl who was kidnapped from an Azerbaijani village when she was eleven years old and then taken to Alexandria, and then to Beirut where she was bought by Mr. Iskandar.

She wasn't Circassian.

Iskandar told his wife he was going to marry the Circassian when his wife saw him embracing her in the kitchen and the young girl sighing in his arms. That was what drove the man crazy. That sigh that came from her eyes. Those eyes whose color Iskandar never could quite define.

Lody went into the kitchen, saw them, and screamed.

He, on the other hand, did not move or become flustered in any way.

"With the maid? You bastard!"

"Shut up!" he yelled, and married Widad.

He said he would marry her, and he did. No one believed him. Iskandar left his house and took her with him. He converted to Islam, gave her freedom, and married her. He lived with her in that little yellow house built of thick sandstone. In the garden were three mimosa trees, a jasmine plant, and an almond tree. He would play the oud and sing to her, drink arak every night, and sing with her by his side. He stopped working, or rather, he went to his shop less often. He disagreed with everyone over her, and loved her.

Lody told her children he was crazy and that men are dogs. "Darwin was wrong," she would say. "Man did not evolve from apes; man evolved from dogs, and Khawaja Muhammad Iskandar is the missing link!"

Iskandar and his new wife went to church every Sunday. No one asked why he was praying there, after converting to Islam, or how. People said the Circassian woman was baptized, but no one really knew.

As for George and his four sisters, the story was a disgrace. The children were brought up in a home whose family had been abandoned by their father, and it stunk of disgrace. The children refused to visit him at first. Their mother forbade it, and they obeyed her, and so it became normal to them not to visit him. But when he became sick three years after his marriage, they started visiting him. They liked that young woman who looked like an enchantress.

George Naffaa remembered that woman who was like a white shadow.

When his father had a heart attack and went to the hospital, he saw her. She was sitting on a chair at the foot of the bed, looking at his father's feet. From time to time she would rub his feet with her hands, tears frozen in her eyes as though she had been crying for a long time, or were about to cry.

That day he saw her.

George said to Amal, whom he would marry five years later, that that day he saw her. At the house, she wasn't there. She was like a spirit. But at the hospital, she turned into something else. It was then that he saw the light: he saw a woman surrounded by light. Her whiteness radiated light—not the kind of reddish whiteness of women from our part of the world—a special whiteness, like a mixture of two shades of white with light shining out from a secret space between them.

Iskandar went home two weeks later, and George would visit him every day, and every day he would see her, walking silently, as if she weren't really walking. He could hear the rustle of her clothes, but not her footsteps nor the sound of her breathing. She was like a nurse. In those days, George and his sisters wouldn't speak to her. They would come to visit their father, and they would catch a glimpse of her; then she would disappear. George would reach out to shake her hand, and she would offer him her small, tender hand, then withdraw to the kitchen, make coffee and tea, and come back. Then she would sit on a chair by the foot of the bed, and from time to time, she would reach over and rub her husband's feet. She always knew when he wanted something even before he asked. If he lifted his head to ask for water, she would hand the glass to him before he made the request. George would watch her, afraid to ask, could a man actually make love to this woman? She was like a spirit. Was it possible to tear away that curtain of silence that surrounded her?

Time passed.

George didn't ask his father anything about her. Once he asked about her memories—her family, the name of her village or city. His father looked at him with his eyes half-closed. That was a habit of Iskandar Naffaa's, to look at his wife, Lody, or his children, with half-closed eyes, whenever he was angry. The father looked at his son with his half-closed eyes to tell him to change the subject, but he didn't. George hadn't come originally to discuss this topic with his father. What he had intended to discuss with his father was the subject of work and marriage. George decided, after completing his degree in management at the American University in Beirut, that he should work and take over ownership of the store. He and his mother had agreed on that. She said he should receive his inheritance right away.

"Your father is sick and could die any minute. Go, get everything. Make sure everything is in your name only. Make sure everything is given to you. Otherwise, when he dies, it will all go to the maid."

George pursued his questions about Widad's memories, so his father answered. "Ask her. I don't know." George didn't ask her. He was afraid she might know, afraid she might answer with things he didn't want to hear.

If he had asked her, he would have gotten the same answer he got from his father, because white Widad didn't know. She knew only what Iskandar knew, and what Iskandar didn't know had been erased from her memory. Even that year she spent in Alexandria as a maid for the Lebanese Khayyat family, who owned two ships that worked the Alexandria-Beirut-Marseilles line, was absent from her memory. It had disappeared from her memory like a ghost.

George stopped talking. His father was lying on the bed, breathing with difficulty.

George mentioned work.

Iskandar opened his eyes and said, "Of course." He told him to start work the next day, that Wadee al-Sukhun would give him everything and teach him what to do. "He's the same as me," Iskandar said. "Treat him like your own father." Then he called for Widad, and she came running. That was when George discovered the secret of her silent footsteps. She didn't wear shoes. She walked around the house barefoot. George saw her wearing shoes only once. Even when she went out she wore rubber slip-ons with no heel, and it was as if she were barefoot. George watched her as she approached quickly, walking as though she were flying.

Widad came.

Iskandar waved his hand. She went out of the room and came back with the papers. Iskandar gave the papers to his son. They were notarized official documents signing over the store and all its merchandise to his son. George took the papers, read them, and bent down to kiss his father's hand, but his father pulled his hand away and turned his face. Iskandar Naffaa was crying.

George left without discussing the other matter. His main reason for coming had been marriage, not the store. He hadn't been convinced by his mother's suggestion. He felt the time was not right, that he couldn't possibly speak to his father about inheritance and death. But Iskandar and the Circassian had already prepared everything. George took the papers and sat silently. He listened to his father weep silently and watched the white Circassian leaning over his feet.

During the many visits George later had with his father, Iskandar never wanted to hear anything about the store. All he wanted to know about was the bookkeeping and distribution of profits between him and his son. Iskandar got better. Dr. Najeeb had told George after his father's third heart attack that Iskandar would not live, that his blocked arteries did not leave him much time. But miraculously, he lived. Lody, who had been waiting for him to die, waiting for the moment when the white Circassian would kneel at her feet and beg her not to throw her out of the house, or beg her to take her back as a maid, waited a long time. She died before ever realizing her dream.

Iskandar lived by the miracle of love. That's what he told his son when he came to talk about marriage. George came early in the morning. That was in September. The ground was wet with that summer rain that opens your lungs to the smell of fresh soil. He arrived, and his father, as he did every morning, was sitting in the garden next to the jasmine, drinking coffee and smoking his narghile. The Circassian wasn't with him. She was inside taking a bath. That's how

Iskandar's summer mornings in the garden were spent—next to the jasmine, drinking coffee and waiting for her to finish her bath. She would come out, her long, wet hair smelling of perfumed soap. Then she would sit next to him silently while he spoke. He would talk about whatever came to mind, forgetting what he had already told her before, retelling his story a different way. He would look at her and see she believed all of it. She believed everything, or at least that's what Iskandar thought. George found out ten years after his father's death that the white woman hadn't believed any of what his father had said. She asked George all kinds of questions about the family's background, the store, everything.

After her husband's death, and long years working in the nursing home, and the whole story of her relationship with Seraphim, the Armenian pharmacist, which George could neither prove nor disprove, George saw Widad in a different light. He saw in her quiet smile a certain cunning, shrewdness, and depth of perception. She questioned him as if she didn't know, but she did know. He told her about his father's work, and about Wadee al-Sukhun and his son Mousa and about the lingerie branch of their business. She listened as though she doubted everything, as though she already knew and didn't need to ask. He found himself drawn in, completely powerless, as he talked to her. It was then that George understood his father's secret. He understood the meaning of those words his father had spoken when he asked for his consent to marry Amal Tabshurani, his classmate at the university. Iskandar did not ask the traditional questions about family background, as Lody did when she tried to persuade him not to marry Amal and look instead for a rich girl. He asked him only about love.

"Do you love her?"

"Of course," George said.

"What do you mean, 'Of course'? I'm asking you about love. Didn't you see what happened when I fell in love—what I did and what happened to me? Do you love her like that?"

"Like what?"

"The way I loved Widad."

"And now you don't love her anymore?"

"We're not discussing her. We're discussing you."

"I don't know," said George. "I know I love her, and I want to marry her."

"Marriage is different from love, my son."

"You got married because you were in love."

"That's right. I married Widad because there was no other solution. But marrying Widad was a love story."

That morning Widad took a long time in the bath. She didn't come out smelling of perfumed soap to sit beside her husband quietly as she did every morning. That morning, she left him alone with his son, and they talked until noon. That day, George got the whole story. He found out that his father had been struck with a kind of madness the very moment he embraced that young, white girl in the kitchen, and he no longer knew how to behave. "It was as though I'd drunk a barrel of arak. I was dizzy—at home, at work—I wanted her. No, not just to sleep with her, not sex, sex is a different matter altogether; I wanted to have her for my own, all of her, everything."

"And now?" George asked.

"Now? What is now?" his father answered. "Who is talking about now? Now she is mine. But I don't know her. When I took her to the Sofar Grand Hotel and married her,

I thought she had become mine, and she had become mine in every sense of the word. But love, my son, means that the other never really becomes yours. In love, the abyss remains forever open. Widad remained an open abyss. I tried to wipe out love with marriage, to tame passion with lovemaking, but I discovered instead the abyss. Maybe it is because she's a stranger, or because I smell in her a strange scent . . . I see her as if . . . as if her very nostrils sense fragrances completely unknown to us. Maybe it is because she isn't a woman. I swear to God she isn't a woman. You don't know women. When you make love to a woman and transport her to the bottom of the sea and leave her trembling with ecstasy, she becomes yours. You become her master, and you feel like you own the whole world—but not her. I swear I never knew if she reached orgasm with me or not. Whenever I asked her, she would shy away and not answer, as though she didn't understand what I meant. Never once did she answer. Never once did she shudder with ecstasy, reach that moment of total extinction in this thing God has created for us. Even when I was certain she had reached orgasm, I was never totally certain because her expression didn't change. Nothing about her ever changes. That's what love is about—it's that opening, that gap, that drives you crazy. I stayed that way—crazy—until the heart attack. I was like someone who searches and searches and never finds what he's looking for. Then I stopped searching. I saw death, and so I stopped. And I love her. I'm not saying I don't love her. I love her, but I don't know. I wiped out the abyss with silence. I wiped out the search with what I had found and what I had owned. This is what marriage is. Before you get married, go and look around."

George told his father he didn't feel that way, that this

was completely different. He said he wanted to marry Amal because he saw her as his wife. He couldn't stand to be without her, he loved her, and he wanted to have children with her.

Iskandar laughed. "You want children. I have five children, but in love I did not have a single child. In love we lived, that girl and I, and we never needed any children."

"That's because she is the same age as your children," George said.

"The same age as my children, true, but she's the same age as my grandparents, too. You don't know anything about age. Age has no meaning whatsoever, it is something external. People have no age. Do you know her age? I don't. But I do know it is ancient and deep. Go ask her. She won't tell you. She doesn't answer. I tried a thousand times to ask her. I told you I didn't ask her anything, but I was lying. I did ask, but she didn't answer. I know she doesn't know the answer. It's inside her, and she doesn't know it. She's like my children, it's true, and she's also like . . . I don't know. Sometimes I think I'm dealing with some strange being. With her, I never felt the need to have children, and neither did she. We lived without children. Children come before love, or after it. But don't confuse love and children."

Iskandar was lying to his son, and the son knew his father was lying to him, but he didn't tell him that. George knew the story of Widad wanting Mirna, and how she cried, how she turned into one big heap of clothes soaked with tears, after Iskandar refused her request to adopt the dark-skinned orphan girl who lived in Zahrat al-Ihsan Orphanage. George knew that talking about love, marriage, and children would lead to nothing, not because his father was lying, but because the subject itself breeds lies. Talking becomes a kind of justification for what you want and the situation you're in. Words, then, no longer express a position. As for the whole thing about age, which was his father's pretext for telling him to wait before getting married to Amal, it was a silly excuse. He listened a long time to his father's views on age and his theory about Widad, who was ageless, and he was becoming convinced. In fact, he was convinced. But then his father came up with that argument that he shouldn't marry Amal because she was the same age as George and it is better for a man to marry a woman at least ten years younger because women are biologically different from men. At that point George got up and told his father it was a ridiculous theory.

"Screw biology. Here I was, convinced that your wife is 'ageless,' so why should my wife have an age?"

"Well, because, I don't know," Iskandar said, and then fell silent, indicating his consent to the marriage.

That whole story about age used to confuse me when I listened to Mary tell me about that soldier she went with near Lucolus Restaurant. He was a seventeen-year-old kid, or that's how old he looked to me, and Mary was thirty-three, the same age as Jesus. When I made love to her on that hammock on the balcony overlooking the sea, I knew that she was thirty-three. I could smell Jesus in her. This is the age that crowns all ages. That's what I've thought for a long time. When I learned about how they crucified Him when He was thirty-three, I thought that I, too, would die at thirty-three. And when I reached the threshold of that age, I was scared to death. He knew that even if He were to die, He would not die, and yet He was afraid. I, on the other hand, didn't know. So how could I not be afraid? That age passed, and I forgot all about the fear of age thirty-three, until Mary went with that tall, dark soldier and left him to die. When she went with him, and I saw them going off into those demolished alleys, I said to myself, "Mary is going to die." I wanted to scream to her not to die; then I heard the explosion, and I saw her coming back, walking confidently and gazing into space as if she hadn't seen or heard anything. She left the young man to die and returned. I knew she had her own special theory about age. She, too, wanted to go because she was searching for that debilitating weakness that overtakes the eyes the moment desire begins. She wanted to see how the soldier would begin. But instead of beginning, he died. Mary didn't tell me anything about such matters. She didn't tell me that desire starts when eyes end. She told me that Marwan al-Aassi didn't love her, because he was attached to his eyes. His eyes led him to look at things. As for the soldier, his eyes were lost before he started eating. She carried the pot of bean stew and sat down next to him. He was hungry, but he didn't eat. He took one bite and said he was full. She ate. She ate with me up there in the demolished restaurant. Then she went downstairs and ate with the other soldiers. I didn't eat, and the soldier didn't eat. But the difference is that he died, and I didn't. This is what bewilders me in my story with Mary. I don't want to tell the story of Mary now. I want to tell about Iskandar Naffaa's views on age. And I agree with him. Age is not only in the hands of God, which of course it is, but it is also an unending question about a past we don't know. White Widad was ageless because Widad was part and parcel of a black cave full of obliterated memories. But Mary was another story. I saw her slipping into her age and afraid of getting old. I used to tell her she was ageless, but she didn't believe me. She kept on not believing me until she went with that soldier and left him to die. That day she came back and told me she believed me. But it was too late. I no longer believed her. Now I saw her like a dress, a dress slipping off of her own white body. I didn't believe the dress, and I didn't believe the body. I didn't tell her I no longer believed her. She saw it in my eyes. She said, "Your eyes no longer . . ." I said I was sick and wanted to shut my eyes so I could see. And I let her go. I saw her going. Maybe she would not have gone. I created the story of the soldier to give her the freedom to go, and she went.   ♦

Mary asked me about the Marys.

She said that what confused her about Jesus was all those Marys around Him.

"And who would you be?" I asked her.

She said that the story of the Marys is Iskandar's story. Iskandar was searching for his own special Mary to help him perform his miracle.

"Remember Cana?" she asked. "In Cana, it was his mother. She was the one who prompted him to perform his first miracle, and at Lazarus's tomb there was another Mary, and at the resurrection, all the Marys were present. Iskandar was searching for his miracle, for his Mary who forgot the salt and disappeared. He wanted to retrieve that salt that drowned the Dead Sea, and drowned the world."

In the Jordan Valley, on the eastern shore of the Dead Sea, I saw that lead gray horizon that enwraps the world. It was as if we were at the end of the universe, where clouds stretch out over the face of the waters and remain transparent, like mirrors scattered over the hills hiding the city of Jerusalem from the valley. The lights of Jerusalem appear in that lead gray color that sways in the sunset as the sun falls asleep inside the salty waters.

The story goes that it was a woman.

In those days, where there was time and it was as if time had not yet begun, a woman called Mary sat. Maybe it was Mary, the sister of Moses and Aaron and daughter of Umran, or maybe it was another Mary, and the world was fading away.

In those days everything died. God had created the world but not salt. There was everything, but there was no salt. Children were born with chapped lips and died. Everything died.

In those days Mary sat in the valley before the sea, and before the sea, she begged God for salt. Seven days and seven nights she prayed. And so God sent her a mill. The mill turned and turned, and the salt poured forth. Mary toiled, and the mill went round and round. The woman cleaved to the mill that turned endlessly, and the salt poured forth.

That is how God created salt. God created the woman, and the woman was the beginning of salt.

That's the story, according to the story.

The woman died. The salt spread all over her face, shut up her eyes, and so she died. The woman died, and the mill tumbled into the sea, and there it remains in the bottom of the sea, turning and turning, around and around; and it will not stop turning until that lead gray twilight returns, the way it was at the beginning of the world. Then the salt will go, and life will return after everything living dies and the world ends.

He said to me, "Mortal, have you seen this?"

Then he led me back along the bank of the river. As I came back, I saw on the bank of the river a great many trees on the one side and on the other. He said to me:

> This water flows toward the eastern region and goes down into the Araba; and when it enters the sea, the sea of stagnant waters, the water will become fresh. Wherever the

river goes, every living creature that swarms will live, and there will be very many fish, once these waters reach there. It will become fresh, and everything will live where the river goes. People will stand fishing beside the sea from En-gedi to En-eglaim; it will be a place for the spreading of nets; its fish will be of a great many kinds, like the fish of the Great Sea. But the swamps and marshes will not become fresh; they are to be left for salt. On the banks, on both sides of the river, there will grow all kinds of trees for food. Their leaves will not wither nor their fruit fail, but they will bear fresh fruit every month, because the water for them flows from the sanctuary. Their fruit will be for food, and their leaves for healing.
(Ezekiel 47: 6-12).

What is the story of the Marys?

Seven Marys were around Him during His short life.

Mary, His mother, who gave birth to Him already wrapped in a shroud. Then He died, and so He cast off the shroud and appeared to His Marys, who didn't know Him at first. He was shining like the radiant sun of justice, and they were all there around Him:

Mary His mother.

Mary the sister of Lazarus.

Mary Magdalene.

Mary the mother of Jacob.

Mary the wife of Clopas.

Mary the mother of John Mark.

The other Mary.

Seven Marys around the sun shimmering over the Dead Sea, whose waters had been restored and become fresh. He was standing among them like a stranger.

I said to him, "Master."

I was standing on the shore waiting for Him, and so I

said, "Master." Then I turned to look and saw the eyes of the Jordanian soldiers behind the hills, not Jesus.

I said to Mary that I didn't see Jesus.

Does Mary know what "Mary" means?

She thinks Mary is just a name like any other name, assigned to women who were around Jesus. But Mary is something else. It is a name full of meanings. "Mary" means "rebellious." It is a Hebrew word that means "rebellious."

Is that why He created Mary as the "new Eve" and surrounded her with Marys?

The first Mary rebelled against Him, according to the story. The second Mary accepted Him. But where is the true rebellion—in refusal, or acceptance?

George told his wife that Widad accepted everything. He gave her little Iskandar. He wanted to give little Iskandar to Widad to make her feel her life had some meaning, but she accepted living without this meaning. "May God keep him to his mother," she said. He asked her to be his son's godmother. Iskandar, the son, had come after a long wait. Iskandar, the father, didn't express his opinion on the matter. He wasn't at all interested in George and Amal's inability to conceive. Widad, on the other hand, was very concerned. She advised George to eat honey mixed with milk for breakfast every morning. "That's the food of the angels," she said to him. She advised him to eat milk and honey and leave the matter in God's hands, to stop going to doctors. And so for twenty years George went on eating the food of the angels, carefully watching the emptiness of his life and the empty space in his wife's womb. Until, at last, Amal became pregnant—suddenly, without any prior indication Amal was pregnant—and didn't stop getting pregnant after that. She had six children: four girls and two boys. Little Iskandar was number five.

When little Iskandar was born, Iskandar senior had already died. George went running to Widad from the hospital, hugged her, and started to cry.

The moment she saw him at the door, and before he even opened his mouth, she asked him, "How is Iskandar?"

"Who told you?" he asked.

"I saw him," she said. "I saw him at midnight. I was asleep and woke up to the sound of his cries. I opened my eyes and saw him."

"He was born at midnight," he said.

George hugged her and burst into tears.

One day before the christening, he went to her and told her he'd chosen her to be the boy's godmother. She accepted, without any discussion, without showing any special joy over it. George thought he was giving her the joy of her life. But she did not move. She agreed, with complete neutrality, as if it were some other woman who had been chosen to be the godmother.

At the christening, which was held at their home because Amal was sick—suffering from the excruciating toothaches she always had after each delivery and which eventually led to the extraction of all her teeth after the birth of her sixth child—Widad stood in front of the baptismal font, wearing her blue dress and white scarf. She took the naked infant from the priest's arms, hugged him close to her chest, and wrapped him in the towel she had draped over her shoulder. She began chanting a hymn, softly. The hymn was not part of the baptismal rite. She sang so softly that one could hardly hear her. The priest stopped chanting his prayers and looked over at her with clear disapproval. He wanted to ask her to be quiet, but he didn't. He let her finish chanting and then resumed his prayers, which he condensed in order to get back to the church where another christening awaited him.

Amal said she looked like the Virgin Mary.

That evening, after everyone had left, Amal told her husband she was frightened when she saw her holding him— as if she were the Virgin Mary, holding her child and taking him to his death.

"Please keep that woman away. I beg you. I don't want her near my son."

George laughed and said that she always hummed that hymn "Give Me This Stranger" because she liked the tune. George explained to his wife, in great detail, the importance of Byzantine music and his theory that music was what had kept the Eastern Church alive in the Arab world, that Byzantine music has the mark of immortality because it gives the impression it is not the work of man. It is a kind of music in which the simpleness of man and the majesty of death are intertwined.

He tried to explain to his wife that Widad sang because she liked to sing, that the intention was the song, not the words.

Amal said she never wanted to see that woman in her house again.

Widad never visited George at his house after that. She refused all his invitations. She was content just to tell him that he and his children were always in her prayers.

When little Iskandar was wounded by shrapnel and became paralyzed, Widad went to him and took care of him for six months in the hospital. She carried him in her arms just as she had done at his christening, and cried just as she had cried, ten years earlier.

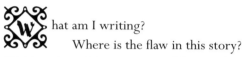 hat am I writing?

Where is the flaw in this story?

Writing about Mary is impossible. Not because I loved her, but because I see her before me now, trembling with fear as we walk through the alleys of the green line that separated Beirut from Beirut. I repeat the names over and over. I was able to count ninety-nine* names. I reached the ultimate number counting the names of friends who had died between the stones of that blood-stained line the war made.

And there was the Circassian mannequin.

Would Emil Azayev understand Widad's tragedy during her last days? Or would he insist on changing the story of Jurji the monk because it is allegedly antisemitic? I heard the story for the first time from an old woman living in Miyyeh Miyyeh Refugee Camp near Sidon. I told him the story the way I heard it. I thought it was a folk tale, and that all the different versions of the story ought to be collected, standardized, and rewritten since the story is part of Palestinian folklore.

The surprise was that while I was doing my research at Columbia University in New York, I came across an article in a newspaper that was called *Al-Quds* about the murder of the Lebanese monk, Jurji Khayri, of Douma, Lebanon.

---

* In Muslim tradition, ninety-nine is the number of names, or epithets, for God.

In the issue dated May 17, 1946, it was written that the monk's body, riddled with ten bullets, was found near the Damascus Gate in Jerusalem. Therefore, what the Palestinian woman had told me was not a folk tale after all. It was an actual event. Here the question arises, what is the difference? How do I deal with the story of the Lebanese monk? Should I revise the Palestinian woman's story, in accordance with Vladimir Prop's prescription with respect to folk tales? Or should I search for the truth?

Mary always made fun of me when I told her I was searching for the truth.

She thought I was only searching for the truth so I could write it, and she believed that when we write it, we betray the truth and turn it into a story.

And Mary was right.

But what else should we do?

"I write therefore I lie," as Ghalib Halasa wrote before dying of a broken heart in Damascus, far away from his "Sultana."

But I am trying not to lie.

"You're just like him," Mary said.

"Who?" I asked her.

"Marwan al-Aassy. Do you know him?"

"No."

She said that he was. "He was in love with me. I was eighteen. He was forty. I fell in love with him, just as any student at the Lebanese University might fall in love with her professor. And he was my professor. I was in love with him a whole year. We would go out to restaurants and have dinner together, and he would recite the most beautiful love poetry to me and sigh. Then I stayed away from him. It wasn't me that went away—the love went away. I got married and had children. Then ten years later I ran into him by chance on the streets of Rome. We went to a restaurant and to some cafes. He recited the same love poems. At the hotel we spent the night in his room. All night long he seemed as if he were going to faint. He held my hand, kissed it. Then a dark cloud spread over his face, and he didn't make love to me. During that year of love, he wrote me a letter every day. He loved me on paper, and when I wanted him and came to him, he collapsed onto his bed like a child who had lost his mother. You are all like that. You love only in your illusions. You are an illusion."

I said, "That's not true," and moved closer to her.

"You only want me because you're not writing about me. You write about others. I know you, all you writers. Your imagination is totally dependent upon fitting others into the illusion of writing."

But I wasn't trying to prove anything to her. I was listening to her story about the white Circassian, but I wanted to write about Jurji the monk. ◆

In those days, the story goes, the Lebanese monk, Jurji Khayri, of Douma, fled from Saint Saba Monastery in Jerusalem. The young Lebanese man's journey from his village of Douma in the Batroun area of North Lebanon, to Saint Saba Monastery, had been long and tiresome. He fled from the rage of his father, who worked in the copper industry, in order to enter the monastery out of admiration for his uncle Saleem, who was an *exarchos. Exarchos,* for those who don't know the meaning of this Greek word, is the highest rank a married priest can attain in the Eastern Orthodox Church. Jurji felt his uncle Saleem deserved to become a bishop, but marriage and children had ruined his chances at that. So he became merely an *exarchos,* ending his clerical career in Damascus, as attendant and nurse to the Patriarch Abifanios the Third, whose old age lasted a long, long time and who came down with all kinds of diseases. Exarchos Saleem held vigil over the Patriarch until he died.

After the Patriarch's death, a new Patriarch was elected, and Exarchos Saleem's services were no longer needed. So Saleem, who had come to be known as Father Jurasimos, went back to his village, where he spent his final days destitute, amidst the constant ridicule of his wife and children, who sneered at his lowly clerical rank, which had led him to become nothing more than the servant to the Patriarch.

Jurji left his village when he was eighteen in order to become a monk in the Organization of the Holy Sepulchre, which manages Saint Saba Monastery in Jerusalem. And there, rather than climbing the spiritual and clerical ladder to bishop, as he had dreamed, he lived a life of depression, loneliness, and persecution. The monastery's administration and most of the clergy were Greeks who hated Arabs. He was persecuted, he and three other Arab monks. They were given all the dirty jobs—washing dishes, sweeping, and mopping. They were not even allowed to do the ironing!

After seven years of suffering, in the fall of 1940, Jurji the monk fled his monastery to live all alone in one of the quarters of Old Jerusalem. At this point, the stories vary. Some say he stayed in Jerusalem and was one of the instigators of the revolution against the British mandate and Jewish settlement. Some say that he didn't live in Jerusalem, but rather that he would go there during Holy Week, that he actually lived in the Galilee and would go back and forth between Palestine and Lebanon as a missionary, living a life of poverty and estrangement. According to a third version, he led a gang in the Galilee, based in the Lebanese village of Cana, and this gang would ransack the smuggler convoys between Lebanon and Palestine and then distribute the loot to the poor. A fourth version is that on Holy Friday, he and members of his gang would kidnap a Jew from Jerusalem and take him to the ancient ruins near the Church of the Holy Sepulchre, and there they would tie him up, tie him to a cross and whip him, as Christ was whipped; and, it was said, they would kill him.

Lots of things were said. No one really knows. Was it true that he and the members of his gang raped young girls? Or was he a God-fearing, abstinent man? According to the story, he was found murdered near the Damascus Gate. And except for the fact of his death, none of the information available about him is certain.

The story, as I told my friend Emil, has nothing to do with antisemitism. Jurji the monk did not torture Jews, or kill them, in the little room he rented in the Christian district in Jerusalem. He was not treated as a monk, but rather as a lunatic. His madness was what made some believe the story of torturing Jews, or the stories of rape. As for his leading a gang in the Galilee, this was the most believable possibility.

Jurji the monk used to carry a big cross and walk through the streets of the Holy City on Great Holy Thursday with the cross tied to his back. Written on the cross, in bad handwriting, was this sentence: "This is the cross of the Arabs, which they will carry one hundred years."

Did Jurji the monk know that the Arab cross would be carried all these years? Was he prophesying? Or was he, as Haj Ameen's group publicized, just a crazy defeatist who had forgotten that Palestine would be returned to its people and that the Jews would not be able to stay one moment after the withdrawal of the British mandate forces?

Had he been killed for that sentence written on his cross? And who would have been the killer? No one knows. Were they the Zionists, or Haj Ameen's group, or was it the "Holy Sepulchre Brotherhood," whose reputation had been ruined by the monk's crazy deeds.

"I don't know," I said to Mary.

And white Widad didn't know why any of this.

The white Circassian did not have any children. She lived alone and died. The story of her death is the story.

But why?

Why do we give death priority and make it the story?

Is it because the end explains the beginning?

And who says death is the end? Does the Lebanese monk's death explain his beginning? Or was his death the beginning which needed to be explained?

Questions, questions—and the answers remained unresolved. I wrote letters to Saint Saba Monastery in Jerusalem asking for information about the monk, but I didn't get any response. So I decided to visit Douma. Perhaps I would come across the truth. And there I found more stories.

I went to Douma. I had never been to that village before. I came to it by way of the Batroun mountains. It seemed as if it were sliding into the valley. From above, from the outskirts of the village of Bshehleh, which extends into the mountains of Tannourine, Douma looks as if it is falling into the valley. Houses, with red rooftops, that drop in a graduated descent, and an endless valley that appears to be part of a bottomless pit. I walked along the main road, which divides the village, and I didn't know how to begin, what to ask, or whom. I didn't have anything specific to go on. All I knew were the names: the name of the monk and the name of his uncle the *exarchos*—but even these I was not sure of because in the church they change the names, the way we did in the Jordan Valley. I said to myself that the best place to start would be the church. There I could find the first answers to my questions.

At the church, the sexton went on about how the church had been built in the nineteenth century and how the Russian consul himself had come to attend the church inauguration. He donated the money for the bell, which was one of the first church bells in Lebanon. He told me about the icons, how they go back to the thirteenth century, and belong to the Hums school of iconography. He told me lots of things I don't remember, because they didn't mean anything to me at the time.

I was searching for the monk, for his story. Was it true that he left Douma and led a gang in the Galilee? Or was the story nothing more than just a story some woman told me at Miyyeh Miyyeh Refugee Camp near Sidon? Was I really searching for the origins of the folk tale, or was I trying to prove to my friend Emil Azayev that the monk was not anti-semitic. In our part of the world, we don't know what *anti-semitism* means. And what's the difference? Emil will never know the outcome of my research, and the monk is no longer a topic now that Jerusalem has been completely occupied and walled in with Israeli settlements. And the story of the cross and all that was written about it no longer have much meaning now that our suffering has extended over half the period the monk predicted. We've been patient for fifty years, so why not wait another fifty, and see what happens? But we won't be able to see. In fifty years Mary will have died, and I, too, and those who will read this story, that is if there is anyone who wants to read it. They will laugh at my naiveté, and the monk's, because the end to our suffering will come only after we pass through an even greater suffering. After it, our grandchildren will be incapable of enjoying its end.

I'll get back to the story.

I went to the church in Douma, and there I listened to the sexton's story about the *exarchos*. He didn't know anything about Jurji the monk. He said he remembered an *exarchos* from the Khayri family. His name was Father Jerasimos. He told me how Father Jerasimos had returned from his long stay in Damascus where he had been the Patriarch's attendant and had died five years later. He said the priest spent the last year of his life alone, after his wife decided to move to Beirut and stay with her two sons who were studying at Saint Joseph's Jesuit University. The priest stayed in the house, all alone. He never went out except to go to church. All of a sudden his back became hunched over, his beard turned white, and he started walking like His Holiness the Patriarch. "God forgive me, but if only you could have seen him, sir. He became . . . how do I describe it? As I was saying, he became just like him, just like the Patriarch, except without the cane. Lord forgive me. Then, God rest his soul, he fell down and couldn't walk anymore. His wife came and visited him for two days, then took off for Beirut and never came back. She said he wanted it that way. Had it not been for God's mercy, he'd have become a laughingstock. She left him, and three days later, he died. Poor man, he spent his whole life serving the Patriarch, and when his own time came, they abandoned him. But God is great. I went to visit him as he was dying. I knew he was dying because he told me so. Then he died, and that's the end of the story."

I didn't want the story of the *exarchos,* or Jerasimos, or I don't know what . . . I was searching for the monk. The sexton insisted there had been no monk named Jurji from that village.

"You know, sir, maybe he changed his name. In the priesthood, they change their names. I don't know any monk by that name. Maybe you need to ask about some other name."

"So what do we do?" I asked him.

"I don't know," he said. "Maybe the best person to ask is the *exarchos*'s cousin's wife."

I said I'd like to visit her.

He led me down alleyways that were like the alleys of a big city. On both sides, there were closed-down shops—or nearly closed down. Apparently the village had once been a city or trade center for the surrounding villages. But its city-like character had begun to fade, and there was nothing left to indicate that character except the arched façades and the coffee shops packed with men, narghiles, and the sound of backgammon tables.

We went to see the cousin's wife, and there we found before us an eighty-year-old woman who constantly swallowed her saliva, as though she were about to swallow her own throat. The sexton told me she suffered from dryness of the throat and mouth, and as a result, she had gotten an infection in her jaws and teeth that had almost killed her.

Um Haleem—that was her name—lived alone in a dark house that reeked of rotten olives. She spoke about the priest and then broke into tears.

She said she was afraid. She said she was afraid of night because it was like a black aba draped around her. She said she suffered from poor eyesight and had started to see the way they see "up there." She pointed up. I understood she meant in Heaven. I didn't ask her how she knew they saw the way she saw, for I was in a hurry to get to the story of the monk, to know what kind of echo he left in his village. Had he become a story here? Or had his story immigrated along with him to Palestine, no longer alive except in the memory of an old woman living in a Palestinian refugee camp near Sidon?

Um Haleem was not in a hurry to get to the story of the monk. She was interested in telling me how they see up there and how, when she developed glaucoma, she had decided not to have an operation. She said she knew the operation wasn't dangerous, but she preferred to keep things as they were—to see how she would see. "Why go backward?" she said. "Death is ahead, and I look ahead. I see Father Saleem. I told him I wouldn't change his name. What kind of a name is 'Jerasimos?' Does he think that later on, up there, I'm going to call him 'Jerasimos?' I'll call him by the name I know—Saleem. He was such a good man; God rest his soul. He died alone and never bothered anyone. And so, my son, this is the end of my story. Did the Patriarch send you? Why, tell me, do Patriarchs die that way? When Abifanios died, Father Saleem sent for me, so I went. The Patriarch was dead. They had sat him on the holy throne. He was embalmed. Later they brought him to the room downstairs. They didn't put him in a grave: they put him in a big room next to the other Patriarchs. I went inside. Good heavens! They were all embalmed, sitting there together, on their thrones, as if they were having a meeting. Oh my goodness. They were all embalmed—one's beard had half fallen out; one's mouth was wide open; one had turned black as coal. I made the sign of the cross over my face and started to cry. Oh how I cried. They thought I was upset about the

Patriarch, but I was crying out of fear. I was scared to death! I was shaking all over, shaking and crying, and that's when the whole thing with my eyes began."

I told her I had never seen the grave of the Patriarchs of Antioch and the rest of the East. I was not interested in that subject. I explained to her I was doing my Ph.D. dissertation on folk stories, and I told her what I knew about the monk from Douma. She looked surprised. Then she insisted the story was impossible because it was simply impossible for a monk to be involved in such political and military activities or to steal. A monk's job is to pray and weep.

"Monks go half-blind," she said. "The monk who doesn't go blind will never become a saint. A monk must weep, and his eyes must go blind so he may take away the sins of the world. How could he have been a monk? No. I've never heard of him."

I was about to leave, and the sexton was looking at his watch as though I had made him miss an important appointment when the woman said she remembered. She said Father spoke about a relative of his who had taken his vows and wore a monk's habit, but she didn't remember him saying anything about Jerusalem. She had only seen that relative once, when he came to visit his uncle in Douma. She said he was short and fat, and his beard was spotted with some kind of oil, and he smelled like a pig. She thought he must have been one of those monks who take a vow never to bathe their entire lives. She couldn't stand to be near him for more than five minutes. He didn't speak, she said: he mumbled. He lived near the well of the Monastery of Saint John Kifteen in the Koura area. He tended the cattle owned by the monastery. She said that was the only time he visited Douma.

"And what about Jerusalem?" I asked her.

"I really don't know, my son. Maybe from Saint John Kifteen he went to Jerusalem. I don't know."

That was what my trip to Douma yielded.

Rather than gather information about Jurji the monk, I found out that in the next world people see blue shadows, just like Um Haleem; that the scene of the embalmed Patriarchs in their tomb scares people; that Father Saleem, or Jerasimos, during his last days started walking the way his master walked and became an invalid just like him; and that Jurji the Monk, for whom I was searching, did not go to Saint Saba monastery, but rather to Saint John Monastery in the Koura. Maybe he returned from the Koura and went to Jerusalem, but no one knows.

Where did the story in the newspaper come from? And how did the monk turn into a story? And who told me the last part of the story, which the Palestinian woman did not tell?

Questions to which I have no answers. All I know is that in Douma I smelled the scent of something burning, that the monk I was looking for was not satisfied to merely carry his cross. He decided to die on it, just as his Lord had done two thousand years before. And I know that the story I told to my friend Emil Azayev was true because I am convinced of it.

Why do I call Emil my friend?

I don't know. Is it because he told me his story? And whenever we listen to someone's story we become friends? So now am I a friend to all of them and a friend to Widad?

Widad, I loved. I loved her just as I loved Mary. I tried to explain to Mary the meaning of love, that when I saw her going to the soldier, walking with him, an obscure feeling came over me, as if I were the one going, as if I had entered into her eyes as a miniature image of a man I used to be. And now here he was, going off to wherever that woman was taking him.

In Douma, I found more stories, but I didn't find the monk. So I decided that the beginning of the story is writing it, that Saint John, when he began his testament with the expression, "In the beginning was the word," he didn't mean the Greek word *logos*, as is widely believed. He meant, rather, the written word. He meant Jesus as a word written on the cross. This is why the monk carried his cross to announce to the Arabs the coming of one hundred years of misery. And for this reason, too, when Widad was tossed onto that green line separating Beirut from Beirut, she looked as though she had been crucified, just like Kamal Nasir, the Palestinian poet whom the Israelis murdered in his home in Beirut in 1972. They nailed him to the ground and poured bullets down his throat.

But Widad was alone.

"She lived her entire life alone," George said to Doctor Najeeb, who tried to restore the white woman's memory.

Now the scene is viewed through George's eyes, and so we see an incomplete picture. George sees the scene in the kitchen when Madame Lody discovered her middle-aged husband holding the young maid. He sees the girl's eyes filled with fear and something resembling tears. He sees Iskandar, holding the maid's hand, leaving the house. Here the image of Widad fades, and the image of Lody appears. His mother went crazy, turned into some kind of lunatic. She collapsed suddenly and began to wail. When she found out Iskandar had become a Muslim and married the Circassian, Lody turned into one big ball of hatred. She started to melt, to shrink, until she became a fine, stretched thread. Her breasts dwindled away, and she became something like a long neck covered with wrinkles.

When Iskandar got sick and everyone thought he was going to die, Lody danced around the house and let out shrieks of joy. She said God was avenging her honor. But, in the end, she died twenty years before her husband. She died still full of spite, as people said. After visiting her sick husband, Lody would come home trembling and fill the house with her screams. She would go into her room and lock the door and wouldn't open it for anyone. What infuriated her most was the way the white Circassian bent over to kiss her hand and the way she sat on the edge of the bamboo chair, head bowed, not saying a word.

At Lody's funeral, Iskandar wept a lot. He stood alone behind the coffin. The Circassian stood in the back with the women. No one looked at her.

Widad did not speak unless her husband asked her to.

She was wearing a white dress, and her head was covered with a blue silk scarf. She walked with her head down like a nun, and didn't speak.

Once she cried.

George and his sisters were visiting their father. Iskandar was lying on his sofa in the living room. He was wearing his embroidered white silk robe and his red Turkish tarboosh, and he had the mouthpiece of his narghile in his hand. The doctors had forbidden him to smoke it, so Widad would prepare it without putting the embers on the tobacco. Iskandar was smoking without smoke, and the narghile bubbled while the children sat with their father. Widad was in her place on the edge of the bamboo chair. Words broke in and out of the silence. And she cried.

George Naffaa remembers that the woman drowned in tears.

He had never seen anyone cry like that before.

A white mass melting into a river of tears. Everyone turned toward her, not understanding. Her whole body shuddered. It was as though she were gasping for her last breaths. She began to convulse. Then the tears flowed, and the sobbing increased. She tried to get up and leave the living room, but she fell to the floor and her weeping began.

George ran to her.

"Leave her alone!" Iskandar shouted.

George retreated. She was thrashing around, all alone, shuddering, the sobs breaking out from deep inside her.

Iskandar raised his hand to tell his children not to move.

She went on like that, weeping out of control for around ten minutes. The father looked at her with unfeeling eyes. The children didn't move. The sound of her wailing subsided and started to fade, sinking deeper and deeper, as if it were drowning.

Then she got up.

She left the living room and went to the bathroom. She washed up, changed her clothes, and went back and sat in her place on the chair calmly, as if nothing had happened.

"She does that," Iskandar said to his children. "She has crying spells from time to time, but it's nothing to worry about."

George told Dr. Najeeb about it when he came to treat her for that horrible illness she got.

"Maybe she has epilepsy," George said.

"No. It's not epilepsy," the doctor answered. "It's something else. God help her. Widad has never been epileptic, and she has not become senile either. It is something else."

And so her crying sickness stayed with her her whole life.

Iskandar Naffaa didn't know when he bought Widad that he would be entering a turning point in his life. He bought her without thinking about it very much. He thought he was solving his wife's maid problem. Madame Lody had a lot of trouble with her maids. Every one of them left within a month, fleeing from her tyranny, stinginess, and arrogance.

Madame Lody felt she had been shortchanged in her marriage to Iskandar. She was from the rich Jalakh family, who were silk traders and had married a commissions merchant who was not from any of the seven famous families of Beirut. Her way of making up for this was to be arrogant toward her husband and tyrannical with her maids, and to speak French. The family crises were always over maids. A maid would come to work, and within a month, she would run away, and the whole house would fall into the whirlpool of searching for a new maid. Iskandar decided that no more maids would enter the house. That was after the incident with the maid Munira from Hauran. Munira was a perfect young woman. That's what Iskandar thought when he saw her with her father at their house, as Lody was negotiating the monthly salary. She was dark, eighteen years old, and knew how to do everything—cook, do laundry, clean the house, prepare the narghile. But Munira couldn't stand staying in Lody's house for more than three weeks. Iskandar was shocked when he saw her attack his wife and start punching her. Then she started smashing everything in sight, like a wild animal. She smashed the good china in the kitchen, then she moved on to the living room and started breaking everything there. She got a hammer and started pounding on the furniture. Everything was broken to pieces. Iskandar stood by, silent. Lody was on the floor, covered with blood.

She didn't even take her clothes with her.

Munira left the house after that battle and never came back. And Iskandar decided to stop getting maids.

"You're to blame for this," he said to his wife. "It's your fault. You have no heart."

Lody moaned that it was his fault and that he had not disciplined the maid because he had ulterior motives.

Lody was heartless with her maids.

She loved the poor. She would donate clothes and food to orphanages. But with the maids, she was a different woman. "A maid is a maid," she would say. She treated them like slaves, made them work day in and day out even if there wasn't anything for them to do. She never let them eat anything but leftovers. She would hit them and wouldn't even give them the old clothes she wanted to donate, or so she claimed, to the poor.

When Iskandar bought the Circassian girl he thought he had found the solution.

He said to Muhammad Lawand, his friend the wholesale merchant, that he wanted to buy a cure for his headache, no matter what the cost. He went with Muhammad Lawand to the America Hotel near the port of Beirut, and there he bought her for five gold pounds. She didn't speak. She had arrived on the ship from Alexandria two days earlier. Her whiteness had turned pale from fatigue and fear, and her eyes seemed empty. She knew only a few words in Arabic in a dialect that was a mixture of Egyptian and Turkish.

He bought her thinking she was Circassian. That's what the man who sold her to him had called her. Iskandar didn't remember anything about him except his bald head that was spotted with oil.

He said she was Widad the Circassian, and she was worth her weight in gold.

Iskandar bought her and took her home.

Widad didn't speak.

Her head was always bent forward a little. She worked all day without a single complaint, expected nothing, and looked at things as though she didn't see.

She had big, cloudy eyes and seemed baffled, as if she were mystified. She walked behind Lody like her shadow, obeying her every command. When Madame Lody hit her, she didn't cry or protest. She was like a shadow, as though she weren't really there. She learned to speak Arabic and understand Madame Lody's French, and Lody stopped complaining about the maids.

"Is this what you do, you ungrateful bitch, after I loved you and treated you like my own daughter?" Lody said to her as she watched her walking behind Iskandar on his way out of the house.

When Lody caught her with Iskandar in the kitchen, the woman didn't believe her eyes. This skinny girl that looked like a shadow was not a woman to Lody. She was nothing. "But men, men are disgusting," she wept to her son George.

The white Circassian didn't understand.

She was in the kitchen, washing dishes. Madame Lody was in bed enjoying the daily afternoon nap, which she took religiously. The children were at school, and Mr. Iskandar was in the living room smoking his water pipe before going back to work.

She didn't see him at first.

She felt him breathing on the back of her neck. She knew who he was from the smell of the Persian tobacco on his breath. She didn't move. She was glued to the floor. He put his hands on her shoulders and turned her around, taking her into his arms. She sighed. She opened her eyes and sighed. Iskandar could see the sighing in her eyes, and all the desires he had never known before were set afire inside him.

He told her he nearly cried from the love he felt for her. Widad is beside him. He is lying on the bed, gasping. He holds her hand and tells her he almost cried that day in the kitchen, and for that he married her.

She puts her hand on his head and asks him to sleep, so he falls asleep.

Whenever she put her hand on his head and asked him to sleep, drowsiness would take hold of him, and he would drift off. That went on for thirty years—his waiting for sleep to come to him through her small hand placed on his head.

Widad grew.

All of her grew. Iskandar saw her growing beneath his touch. Her breasts became round, and she became taller and more beautiful. Her hips filled out, her hair grew longer and longer. He wouldn't allow her to cut it. Everything grew and changed; everything but her hands. Those two hands remained small and tender, beckoning him to sleep.

When Lody came into the kitchen, Iskandar had no idea where that spur-of-the-moment action of his was about to lead him. He had approached the young girl on a whim, the way he had done with all the maids. He didn't have sex with them; he just liked to play around. That's what he would tell his friends when they sat drinking arak—that he had snatched a kiss, or a squeeze, little things like that, just for the physical thrill. He went after this girl just as he had gone after the others. That he would answer his wife the way he did, was the furthest thing from his mind. It was not the first time Lody had caught him in a compromising position with one of the maids. Usually, he would claim he was hitting her or rebuking her for something. Lody understood of course and would just let it go, becoming ever more convinced that sex was vile and men were filthy, and in bed, she would be a block of ice.

This time, though, Iskandar did not claim he was rebuking the Circassian. He was completely taken by that water in her eyes, by that sigh that came out from deep inside her. He held her, heard his wife's footsteps, and didn't let go.

He hugged her tighter and pulled her closer to him, and began smelling her all over. Lody saw him sniffing her, the way an animal sniffs out its female before copulating. The girl sighed, surrendering, while Iskandar melted away, losing his ability to control himself.

When his wife screamed, her voice came forth as if from a deep well. The sound of it had absolutely no effect on him. He took the girl by the hand, left the house, and married her.

As for Widad, here lies the question.

No one knows what she felt, or what she thought, or what she wanted. She walked behind him and went where he took her.

Did she see things then the way she saw them in the end? Did she know? Did the roads she traveled between Beirut and Sofar mean anything to her?

No one knows.

Iskandar didn't tell the story to anyone. He took her and went to Sofar. They stayed in the Sofar Grand Hotel in the mountains, where he turned her into a married woman. Then he brought her back to live in their new house surrounded by the fragrance of mimosa and jasmine.

During their whole life together, he never asked her a single question about her homeland or her family. Whenever he saw her crying, and she was always crying, he would just leave her, drenched in her tears, and not ask. And she never said anything.

She learned to speak Arabic very well. She learned to read and write on her own. She would figure out letters here and there from magazines and newspapers and ask Iskandar, who would smile and teach her. She got to be just like everyone else and lived like everyone else. She was part nurse, part nun. She stayed with Iskandar, took care of him, looked after his health, and served him. She would place her small hand on his head, and did not leave.

Iskandar lived his life as a lover, and as any lover might be, he was afraid of this white young girl. He imagined her leaving him and was afraid. That's how he saw her during his sickness, disappearing from his life the way she had entered it, passing through the same white wall she had come from and leaving. But he knew she had no place to go to. Nevertheless, he didn't leave anything to her in his will. He knew that when he died Widad would return to her country. Iskandar died, but Widad did not return. She stayed in the same house, living the kind of life she had grown accustomed to with her husband, as though he had never died. One of her neighbors, who was her seamstress and only friend, said she once saw her opening the closet and talking to her husband's clothes, which she kept hanging in the closet. Widad would wash them, and iron them, and put them back in their place. ♦

Widad learned to read and write. Every day she would go to Zahrat al-Ihsan Orphanage where she worked as a volunteer. Iskandar did not object. He thought it would help her adjust to her new life. She wanted to help the young orphan girls, but she discovered that they had been turned into maids of a sort, so she would work with them like a maid. She would come every day at ten in the morning, after finishing her housework, and work hard at the orphanage until two in the afternoon. Even when her husband's sickness worsened and she had to spend most of her time at home, she didn't stop working at the orphanage.

Only once did she request something from Iskandar.

Always, when Iskandar finished drinking his nightly allotment of three glasses of arak, he would start kissing her and shout, "Ask for anything. All you have to do is say the word." She never asked for anything. She refused to have a maid, refused gold and diamonds and the piece of land he wanted to sign over to her. She didn't take anything, and when she asked him for Mirna, he refused.

She asked her husband only once to allow her to adopt one of the girls from the orphanage. He refused. He said he already had four daughters, and he couldn't possibly adopt another.

That day Widad cried. She kneeled on the ground and kissed his feet. He was sick with bronchitis. She knelt and cried out, "Please. I beg you. I will do anything for you, Master, anything." Just let me have Mirna." He said no.

Widad cried. From that day on, the white Circassian would drown in her tears. Iskandar got used to her crying.

The doctor asked Iskandar's son about Widad's friends.

George Naffaa started to think his memory was betraying him. He was only one year younger than Widad. The war, and aging, and his sick son, and the worries, all caused his memory to snap. He found difficulty remembering names of people and places, but this did not affect his mental abilities at all, nor his abilities to run his business affairs, despite the difficult circumstances of the war.

George told the doctor he didn't know anything about her friends. He did visit her regularly after his father's death, but he knew nothing about her. He told his wife she was a noble woman. He went to see her three days after his father's burial, to discuss the inheritance with her. She said no. "You can have everything, son. All I want is a quiet life." She signed over everything to them and insisted on giving up her share of the very house she was living in. She said she would be joining her husband soon, and there was no need to go through complicated legalities to transfer the inheritance.

But she lived thirty years more.

She said to George she would return soon, and so he understood she was talking about joining her husband. But she didn't return. She remained in that house, and went on living as she always had. One thing changed, and it had nothing to do with her husband's death: it had happened before he died. Widad stopped going to the orphanage after Mirna—the girl who had been her sole request of her husband—got married. When Widad didn't find Mirna among the other girls, she left everything and ran over to see Sister Barbara, the Mother Superior, and asked about Mirna. The nun answered that they had married her off and she had left. The nun said it was better that way. She didn't tell Widad the name of the husband nor where the girl had gone.

Widad stopped going to the orphanage. She spent her time at home and never went out. For three years. One year before her husband died, and two years afterward. Then she began working at the nursing home.

George Naffaa thought she was having an affair with Mr. Seraphim, the old pharmacist who lived alone with his wife and no children. After his wife died, he closed his pharmacy and decided to live in a room at the nursing home. Widad would visit him in his monk's cell (that's what he called his room, on whose walls he had hung twenty Byzantine icons). She would care for him for free, as part of her work at the home. Then it was rumored that she was his girlfriend. George did not rule out the possibility, but he didn't dare ask her about it. When Mr. Seraphim died, Widad walked behind the coffin like the men. She stayed up all night with him in the church before he was buried, but she didn't cry.

"Who is this woman?" Mary asked me.

We were walking in the middle of all that destruction, as though we were walking out in space. The vast space of destruction makes you feel like you are suspended on a balcony separated from everything.

She said women are women. Widad was searching for her name but didn't find it. So she returned to where she must return.

Samia did not return.

"Samia goes wherever she's going," I said to Mary. I said to her that Samia was searching for Faysal when she held my hand in front of the grave, and that love rose up into my eyes, that love that didn't dare take the form of words, yet she pointed to the grave of Ali Abu Tawq. And Ali could be Faysal. But not me. Why did she call me Faysal? And why did I respond when she called me by someone else's name? Is it because I am merely a passing lover, or passing visitor? Did I keep quiet because I am just a passerby, or do passersby keep quiet?

"Life is just a passing visit," Widad said to her husband's son. "It's not worth the trouble. Take everything, son. I don't want anything."

That day, George kissed her with tears in his eyes. He began visiting her once a week. He would spend a few minutes with her and then go. He would ask her if she needed anything, and she never did. He would come at nine o'clock in the morning every Saturday. The coffee would already be prepared. He would drink his coffee and go, while she remained in her place like a shadow, sitting on the edge of her chair, her blue scarf covering her hair and her head half-bowed down.

Nothing changed.

The war with all its brutality and strangeness did not change a single thing in that woman's life. Actually, yes—once everything changed. George's house was hit by a 155 millimeter projectile. The house was almost completely demolished. No one was injured, except for little Iskandar. When Iskandar got hurt, Widad broke all the rules and went to see him in the hospital. She stayed by his side for six months, not leaving him for a second, day and night. She took care of him as though she were a nurse, never asking anything and never tiring. When he got out of the hospital, paralyzed, Widad went back home. She never visited him at his house. She would ask George about him without actually mentioning his name. She would ask without waiting for an answer, and George never answered. He would nod his head while she poured coffee for him, and he would drink his coffee while she herself would not drink any.

Then came the end.

Widad got sick. Her feet became heavy, and she preferred to stay in bed. Then one morning, that strange thing occurred. Suddenly, Widad forgot language. Widad the Circassian, who spoke Arabic and no other language, forgot her language.

George Naffaa told the story of how she went through two horrifying experiences during her illness—the experience with her hair and the experience with her language.

Her white, wavy hair that cascaded over her shoulders, started falling out. Her hair problem bewildered everyone. Clumps of hair would fall out onto her shoulders, and she would brush them away and throw them onto the floor, showing no sign of concern or fear.

George Naffaa, who started visiting her every day while she was sick, expected every morning to find her completely bald. But he would find her with hair still on her head. When she raised her head to greet him, the white hair would fall onto her shoulders, and she would dust it off and go on speaking as if nothing had happened.

Then language died.

She refused to go live at her husband's son's house, and she refused to go to the hospital. She looked at George with contempt when he suggested the nursing home. She even sent Dr. Najeeb Canaan away, who was a close friend of her husband's, saying she didn't want anyone.

Then she died.

No. She didn't die.

Before she died, language died, and she forgot everything.

George came to see her in the morning as usual, bringing food and clean clothes. She looked at him dumbly, as though she didn't know him. He asked how she was doing, and she answered him in a language he didn't understand. He asked again, and again she spoke, and the words were not words. George didn't understand. He was scared. He didn't know what to do.

"What's wrong, Mother?"

That was the first time he ever called her "Mother."

The mother was talking and talking, in some other language. George didn't understand a single word.

George sent for Dr. Najeeb, who called the hospital for an ambulance. She was taken by force to Jaitawi Hospital. There, while trying to prevent her from getting out of bed, one of the nurses discovered the woman was as strong as a bull, and spoke a language similar to Turkish.

The Armenian nurse Taleen knew a few Turkish words from her grandmother who had fled Turkey during the great massacre that took place during World War I. Taleen said to George that Widad was speaking a language similar to Turkish, and about only one subject—her childhood. She spoke about her childhood in that distant land, before she was kidnapped and sold in Beirut, and before she married Iskandar Naffaa.

Before she escaped from the hospital, Dr. Najeeb visited her and tried to help her regain her language or make her remember her life in Beirut, but to no avail. The doctor said it was a well-known condition in geriatric medicine, in which the brain covers up the present, blots it out, and brings back the past. Even acquired language goes, and nothing remains on the surface of the brain except the memory of childhood and the language of childhood.

"She's forgotten everything, as though she never was," George said to his wife as he cried.

Widad was.

At five o'clock, on the morning of May 9, 1976, Widad escaped from the hospital. Early in the morning, when sleepiness weighed heavily upon the nurses' ability to keep watch, Widad put on her clothes, left the hospital, and never came back. Three days later a body was found on Damascus Road, near the entrance to Birjawi Quarter. She walked alone, and then she died. Maybe she was searching for her homeland, which had awakened in the hollows of her memory. Suddenly, her memory woke up, opened up, revealing the bottom of a deep well, and then the grave swept it to where there is no return.

Iskandar Naffaa, her husband, did not know that this Circassian woman was not Circassian at all and that throughout her long life in this city, she was a stranger devoid of memory. He felt she had been created from his own rib, that she belonged to him alone. During his long illness, he felt as though he were her father and her husband and had created her from nothing and turned her into a woman.

And when she forgot everything, she remembered everything.

"Where is the truth?" Emil asked me.

Is the truth of white Widad her life as we tell it now? Or is it the life she did not live? Or neither?

Amid the whistling bullets, the white woman fell. Beirut's memory was being torn apart and scattered over the thousands of opposing guns.

"Man forgets," as the Arabs say. But no, when he forgets, he remembers. This is how we are; we remember and don't forget. After all, weren't these wars exercises for the memory? They say war is an exercise in forgetting, since if we did not forget these slaughterhouses we so vigorously enter into, the rebuke of a guilty conscience would kill us. But conscience, gentlemen, is another matter altogether. It requires new thinking.

Widad, having awakened from her long Beirut nap, went to the only place where there is memory. She went to the war. There she did not find her village, the name of which she didn't know, and neither did anyone else, and she didn't find her mother, or brothers, or sisters. There she found us, carrying our guns and our blood. There the white Circassian drowned in her blood, and her story came to an end, like a story in a book.

Widad came to an end, the way stories come to an end, and along with Widad went her jumbled memory with its mixed-up languages. In the end, she became a story of silence. Widad was always silent—a woman wrapped in silence and draped in a cloud of sadness you could read in her eyes.

I told this story to Salman Rushdie.

"It would make a good novel," he said.

"I know," I said, "but I'm afraid of writing it."

He didn't ask me why I was afraid, for writers know that writing is the ultimate encounter with fear. The page is the page of fear—not fear *for* the story, fear *of* the story. We are afraid the story will swallow us, make us marginal, blot us out rather than push us into the forefront, make us vanish rather than appear, and thus make us become a piece of a story. Where it leads us and how it finishes with us, we don't know.

I told Salman Rushdie this story when I met with him in London in 1988, before his book *The Satanic Verses* was published and writing turned a corner where words became like a rope dangling near the well of death. I wanted to tell him the story of the village doctor, but instead I told him the story of the white Circassian.

"And what about you?" I asked him.

"What about me?" he said.

"How do you relate to language?"

He smiled slyly, as if he knew to what exile his words would eventually lead him.

I asked him how he relates to his native Urdu. He told me he came to England when he was six years old, and that in his dreams he spoke in English and Urdu, but eventually English took over.

"Not now," I said.

"When?" he asked.

I told him we could write a novel about an Indian writer who comes to London at age six and writes his novels in English. At a certain age he gets that memory sickness, and so he forgets English and goes back to speaking his native tongue and can't read his own novels.

"But I haven't forgotten Urdu, so I can't then remember it, as your Circassian heroine did. I chose English consciously." He talked to me about how he relates to the English language and how he felt he had control of it.

"Language is like land," I said to him. We can occupy other people's languages just as we can occupy their land. But the question is who are we? Are we running from one enemy to another enemy? Can we accept telling a story, and rather than have the stories we write be read, become instead a story ourselves?

I remember Salman Rushdie gave me a copy of his *Satanic Verses* manuscript that day. We were discussing his novel *Shame,* and I was telling him what scared me about Third-World literature was its peculiar tendency to turn into a page out of history and become classified in the West under the category of "oddities whose problems have no logical solutions."

I don't remember exactly what we talked about, but I remember we drank some wine. In the end we discussed the village doctor, which is another story Mary told me, or I told her; I don't remember anymore. I was, like any other reader, surprised by the story of "The Perforated Sheet" in Salman Rushdie's novel *Midnight's Children*. In Rushdie's story, Dr. Aadam Aziz falls in love with his patient Naseem through the hole in the sheet. The story goes that the girl would call for the doctor whenever she had any pain. The doctor would make his visit under the supervision of her strict father, and examine her without examining her. The father found a strange way to show his daughter's body to the doctor. She would stand behind a sheet and present through a hole in the sheet the part of her body that was hurting her. She kept getting sick, and the doctor kept making visits, and the whole matter ended up with the doctor having seen every part of Naseem through the hole. Dr. Aadam fell in love with the girl through the hole in her sheet and married her so he could connect the holes and his eyes could put together the pieces of her body.

When I told this story to Mary, she told me the story of the village doctor. I already knew the story because I had heard it from a cousin of ours who still lives in al-Munsif, a village in northern Lebanon. My family is originally from that village. We migrated from there three hundred years ago for unknown reasons. That's what my father told me, and I believed him, because I need to have a village of origin. When you live in Beirut you need to secure the idea that Beirut is a choice, not a city you belong to. You choose Beirut because you want to be from Beirut. That is the secret of Beirut that everyone who has lived there knows.

In that village, sixty or more years ago, there lived a traveling doctor, who was one of the first graduates of the French Medical Institute in Beirut. His name was Dr. Lutfi Barakat. Stories about the doctor's personal life, and his numerous relationships with women, and his children's claims that they have illegitimate siblings in many villages in Mount Lebanon do not concern us here. What is of interest is how he used to examine his female patients. In those days, the story goes, doctors were not allowed to look at a woman's body even if she were on her deathbed. That was the custom of the people of the Mount Lebanon area, no matter what the sect. It was considered a violation of honor. And this doctor of ours, who rode from village to village on his donkey, carried a little figurine of a naked woman in his satchel. I asked my father to take me to al-Munsif so we could search for the figurine. Maybe we would find it at the home of one of his children or grandchildren. But my father, despite his respect for literature, believed an author should be like Kahlil Gibran and compose poetry and stories from his imagination, not go from place to place looking for them the way I do. "A writer is not a traveling salesman," my father said. "He is the one who writes the things for people to say. He doesn't steal people's ideas and say it's literature." And he said that he knew nothing about al-Munsif except for what he saw during a visit he made forty years ago and that my visiting that remote village wouldn't help me to find the figurine or the story.

The doctor carried a little figurine of a naked woman in his satchel, and along with it a short, thin bamboo rod. He would enter a sick woman's home, place the figurine on the table while she lay in bed moaning, and he would ask her to relax a little and tell him where she felt pain. And the patient, like all patients in a lot of pain, would not be able to specify where the pain was. The doctor would ask her to open her eyes wide, and he would explain that he was going to pass the rod over the figurine's body and that she should tell him when it touched the part of her body in pain. This method had a magical effect on Dr. Lutfi Barakat's female patients.

When the patient would see the little rod gliding over the naked figurine, she would start moaning and screaming. He would take away the rod and ask his patient to relax a little because no matter where he touched the figurine she would start screaming, making it impossible for him to determine with any precision where the pain was.

After the first round of moaning and screaming, the doctor would give her a glass of water and tell her to drink it slowly. Then he would sit on a chair and smoke a cigarette, taking a long time to roll it and smoke it, allowing the patient to feel at ease. He would not ask her parents to leave the room, but with a look from him that pierced through the white smoke of his cigarette, they would go out and leave him alone with his patient, leaving the door ajar.

Then the doctor would start again. He would slowly pass the stick over the naked figurine in front of him. The patient would start moaning quietly as the rod went on. At this stage the doctor would glide it from the head to the feet, slowly and gently, and let his patient moan. Then, when he reached the right spot, she would scream in pain. She would scream like a wounded animal, and the doctor would press hard on that spot, the rod quivering beneath his fingers, and the screaming would intensify—screaming, and panting, and teeth chattering, as though she were giving birth. Then he would remove the rod, and the woman would quiet down and break into a feverish sweat. He would tell the parents to wrap her in heavy blankets, and he would leave the room— he, and the figurine, and the rod, and the satchel—and he would prescribe some medicine. The doctor knew at this point that his patient was better, as soon as he saw her shivering and sweating all over. He would prescribe something for her because he had to, in order to satisfy her illusion that medicine would cure her. But he knew she was better and that he could leave feeling at ease.

I wanted to say to Salman Rushdie that the difference between his story about Dr. Aadam and Mary's story about Dr. Lutfi Barakat was only a linguistic one. In his story there is an Eastern woman telling the story, in her language and from her point of view, and so she covered herself with a perforated sheet, allowing the doctor to fall in love with her piece by piece. In Mary's story, the narrator is an Eastern man. The bamboo rod is a symbol much like the symbol of the hole in the sheet. But what if the two symbols were to meet? What if we were to put Dr. Lutfi's bamboo rod in the hand of Dr. Aadam? Would the story be possible? The story is only possible when one of the pieces is a symbol; otherwise the story becomes a reality, an unbelievable reality something like the kind of Third-World literature we have these days.

I don't remember what Salman Rushdie's reaction to the story of the village doctor was. I was busy asking about language and occupation and migration. I saw him before me as a possible hero for his own story. I saw him the way I saw white Widad. But here, once again, Widad didn't choose her life, she chose her death. But, we who claim we have chosen our lives will not be able to choose our deaths. Death will come and enwrap us without our knowing it. Which is the better choice—to choose how we live, or how we die?

I won't say I don't know, for I have said that so many times in this novel. What I do know is that I said to Salman Rushdie that his choice will lead him to end up as a probable hero in one of his novels, and I didn't know that what was awaiting him in these times was the worst of all the destinies of all heroes. What was awaiting him was the danger of death, of writing, of freedom.

Rushdie got up and gave me the *Satanic Verses* manuscript. I said good-bye to him and left. One year later his novel was published, and you know the rest of the story.

The story, then, is what we tell.

We find stories tossed in the streets of our memory and the alleys of our imagination. How can we bring them together, to impose order on a land in which all order has been smashed to pieces?

Who are we to tell stories?

And why haven't these stories, or ones like them, been told before? Why is it that in all Maroun Abboud's stories we do not find a single one like the story of Dr. Lutfi Barakat? I didn't make up the story, and neither did Rushdie when he wrote the sheet story, and neither did Naguib Mahfouz when he wrote the story of Mr. Ahmad Abd al-Jawad. The story exists, whether Mary tells it, or I tell it. There is no difference.

Why didn't we tell our stories before this war?

Is it because we didn't know how? And how can that be when we have Maroun Abboud, the master of knowledge and story telling and language and narrative? Or is it because the outward appearance of things wiped out the stories, pushing them into the realm of forgetfulness?

Once again, I don't know.

But I can assure Mary, and I am telling all this to her because she is in front of me, and next to me, and around me. I can assure her that I see the figurine in front of me. It is twenty-five centimeters tall, white, or slightly off-white, as though it's made of ivory. She is standing sideways. Her right leg is bent a little at the knee, her eyes are small, oriental-like in shape, and she is standing on the table, waiting.

The figurine was asleep inside Dr. Lutfi Barakat's satchel,

next to the short bamboo rod she was waiting for, so she could hear the screaming and wailing.

Is it Mary sleeping next to me? Or is it a long dream?

In those days, stories were not like stories.

Mary said she didn't know that all of this would become a story. "It's important that we not know," she said, and then she fell asleep. I took her into my arms and let her drift off to sleep. Her eyes went away, closing shyly. I got closer to her white body. She went completely limp, as though she were expecting me to lay my head on her as though she were a pillow. I took her in my arms, and the fires ignited. Her body was on fire, as though she had a high fever.

In those days, when I laid my head on Mary, I wasn't sure if it was Mary I was lying on, or the white Circassian. Was she the story, or the one telling it to me? And she asked me, "Is love the story of love?" and asked me to tell her a story.

That night I wondered about Faysal's dream. The dream occupied my thoughts as I walked through the demolished alleys of Shatila. The houses were leaning over each other, as though they were embracing each other, and I was walking on the mud and dirt, looking for Samia and asking about Faysal.

"Faysal died," Samia said, holding my hand as she led me to Ali Abu Tawq's grave.

And Faysal, who died, what did he see in his dream that September night of 1982, when he was shot and lay down among the corpses of his mother, brothers, and sisters?

When he told it to me, I was in the hospital. I was searching for him. No, I wasn't searching for him; I was searching for the story and the heroes.

How should I describe him?

A young boy, eleven years old, olive skin, like all Palestinians, or as we imagine Palestinians to be. He looked like those boys who throw stones in the streets of Gaza and Nablus. But he was devastated. Have you ever seen a devastated boy? Usually we use the word *devastated* to describe an old man who has suffered some kind of tragedy. But this boy was devastated, and yet he didn't look like an old man—a plain, olive face, small eyes that danced around his face, a straight nose, full, sagging lips, and words.

Faysal spoke a lot of words.

He spoke, and I listened to him as though I were dreaming. I don't know why his voice seemed that way, as though he weren't there, like a voice in a dream. In dreams we don't hear voices, we remember them when we wake up, but when we hear them, it means the dream is over.

He told how he laid his head on the corpses so he wouldn't die.

"The armed men came in and started shooting. The sound of the gunfire was really loud. First there was the sound, and then the bodies started to fall, one by one, and pile up on top of one another. We were heaped on top of one another." Faysal said, "The whole family was sitting watching TV, when the flare bombs the Israeli Army was firing started falling. Then the Phelangists came in and started shooting."

"I didn't see their faces," Faysal said.

Faysal didn't remember the faces, but he remembered the bodies. "The bodies were heavy," he said. He remembered the weight of his little sister's body, who was seven years old, and how her body dried out and became like a log. After many long hours—Faysal thought he might have slept some of the time or passed out from his wounds—he escaped. He ran to the main street, to the flies and the corpses and the stench. He slept from one to five o'clock in the morning; then he started running. When he saw the foreign reporters, he crouched on the ground and didn't speak.

This is how truth comes out of dreams.

When Faysal dreamed of the return to Palestine, he saw his homeland deserted and found himself alone. And when he laid his head on the bodies of the dead, he ran to the street of corpses, and when he returned to Shatila to fight the war of the camps that lasted three years, and to live through the siege, he was searching for a way to go to Palestine. Palestine came to him in 1987, in the form of a bullet in the head, and a grave in a mosque.

"Is this really the truth?" I asked Emil Azayev.

Did I tell him Faysal's story, or did I quit after explaining to him that the story of Jurji the monk is worth writing? I'm not sure, but I did tell him about Wadee al-Sukhun, Iskandar Naffaa's business partner, who immigrated to Palestine in 1959. I told him how he sold everything, and quickly, in order to be with his only son, Mousa, or Moshe, as they called him at home. Mousa finished high school at L'Alliance High School in the Wadi Abu Jameel district in Beirut, and left the country. He disappeared from the house, leaving a letter for his father saying he was immigrating to Israel. That day, Wadee al-Sukhun was devastated—not because he was against immigrating to Israel or was against the Zionist Plan. No, it was a different problem. The man was settled in Beirut. He had reached the end of his life's journey, and now in his late seventies, he was being asked to leave and start his life over again.

When George Naffaa came to buy everything, there was a lot of hatred. Wadee al-Sukhun shuddered with hatred, and so did George. And suddenly there was no longer room for any emotion, except for that feeling of being strangled.

"You," Wadee al-Sukhun said, and he didn't use the expression, "my son," as he had in the past. "You people want to buy everything for nothing."

He was in a hurry to sell and to leave.

George Naffaa, who bought everything, and not for nothing as al-Sukhun accused him, but for a reasonable price considering the deteriorating economy in Lebanon after the civil war in 1958, was also in a hurry to buy and get out of that house.

Wadee al-Sukhun left, and people lost touch with him. Even his daughter Rachel, who was married to a Muslim from Beirut named Kamel Arnaoot, didn't know anything about him, or so she claimed. Wadee al-Sukhun died in Tel Aviv, three years after arriving there. His wife stayed with her son, who was an engineer in Haifa.

"He hadn't expected to become nothing, just become a common retired man," the mother wrote to her daughter. And Rachel didn't tell anyone about her family's life in Tel Aviv and later in Haifa. Even her husband didn't bring up the subject.

Rachel's story is different from the white Circassian's.

Rachel didn't have a story. People forgot even her Jewish background, and no one reminded her of it. As for Widad the Circassian, she ran through the streets of Beirut as if she were running through the alleys of her memory. When she decided to return to her far away homeland, she went to the demarcation line, and there she died, and her body was not discovered for three days.

What am I writing?

Why does the story of Wadee al-Sukhun seem cloudy, and never-ending? This is the paradox of stories' endings. Wadee al-Sukhun's problem was not with his business partner's son, who had become his partner and friend, and like a son to him, if not dearer as he used to say. His problem was with his own son, Mousa. Mousa was searching for the beginning. He spoke about the "Land of Israel," as the beginning of all things, the beginning of life and of freedom—personal freedom, freedom with women, freedom from Beirut, freedom from the strict Jewish traditions that pervaded their home, and freedom from his father. His father agreed with him on the necessity of "returning" and on everything else. But his father didn't want to go because he couldn't. He was, as his son said to him once, waiting for death and nothing else.

Wadee didn't understand that expression, "the goal in life," his son used constantly. "The goal in life is to live, there is nothing more important than living," he said to his son.

His son went to live in Israel. The al-Sukhun house became empty. Moshe left a short note and left. His father couldn't stand life after that. He sold everything and left, and left nothing in Beirut except his daughter Rachel, who married a Muslim.

Wadee al-Sukhun vanished, and so did any news of him. George Naffaa lost track of him. In July of 1985, after sixteen years had gone by, Rachel came to see George. He knew who she was immediately, as though the years had never passed. Rachel came with the beginning of the war, and before George Naffaa's house was destroyed by the bomb and his son became paralyzed.

Rachel asked George for money in order to go to her daughter Andrée in Paris. She said she couldn't take it anymore, that she had been living alone since her husband's death, and that the war . . . George didn't ask her if she was going to go there. He asked her about Mousa and about her parents. She had tears in her eyes as she took the money George had put in a small envelope, and she told him of her father's death, and about his stroke and how he couldn't speak. For two years he remained mute before he died.

She told him how she traveled to Cyprus when she found out he was sick and called him from there. She spoke with her mother and Mousa. Wadee was unable to speak. They put the phone to his ear so he could hear his daughter's voice, but he couldn't answer.

He died in Tel Aviv just as he had lived in Beirut—silent. Wadee al-Sukhun, the short, round-headed, dark man with eyes that gleamed, didn't talk. He whispered. His friends and customers were engulfed by whispers. He was a man of few words. He would come near you to talk to you and make you understand without having to listen to his words.

Rachel took the envelope and thanked George quietly, as though she were whispering. He said good-bye to her and told her she was like a daughter to him and could always depend on him for anything. She answered, whispering, and so George didn't hear anything but "thank you."

Where is the flaw in this story?

Is it in the comparisons, and I'm not comparing? Things evoke associations with other things and intermingle, forming the image of the mirrors that envelop this Dead Sea on whose shore we stood, Mary and I, and saw the stories dip into its lead-gray horizon.

I wanted to swim. I wanted to walk on water, but this time I didn't dare. This time I was afraid of drowning. I was afraid of the soldiers' eyes who were encamped on the two shores of the sea. I was afraid of the sea.

Was Jesus afraid on the cross?

Why did they dress Him in sheep's clothing and leave Him sacrificed, amid the gods. He was at the feast of the gods, and He was the blood that covered the sky.

He went to the white clothes and put them on in order to be the last of the dead and the first of the living, in order to be the beginning and the end, and so He became a word.

What did He say to His God when He cried out on the cross?

I ask, and Jesus doesn't answer.

I ask, and the sea surrenders itself between the two shores of salt, and the lights from the Israeli settlements pierce the lead-gray color covering the surface of the sky.

I ask, and the Lord lays His head on His Marys, and dies.

And I am alone.

I, and you, and He.

Alone we face this dam of eyes swollen with anger.   ◆

The story is the real question.

And the story is that we are all searching for our story, while claiming to be searching for the truth. We find the truth, and so we lose the story, and start all over again.

Wadee al-Sukhun didn't have a story. He exchanged his missing story with hatred, thereby filling in the empty moments he spent with his partner's son, when he sold him the house and his share of the agency and the store. Wadee al-Sukhun didn't hate George. He just didn't find anything else to feel but hatred, as he was being uprooted from Beirut in order to go to where he must return.

What is the difference between him and the Russian woman Albert Azayev married?

Emil said he immigrated to New York when he realized that justice is impossible. He ran away from the impossibility of obtaining his own justice only to find the justice of others, the impossible justice of others, that exists in America.

In Israel he served in the "Defense Army" during the October War of '73, or the Yom Kippur War, as he called it. After that he was sent to Gaza. He said he decided to leave the country when he saw that old man crawling on his knees, on his hands and knees, backward, afraid he would be shot in the back.

"When you are there you have to choose between the old man and the man carrying the rifle. You can't not choose. I am the rifle, and he is the old man, so what do I do?" After his army service was over, Emil decided to immigrate to America. The choice between two truths led him to "the American dream," or "the American lie," as he called it.

Emil stood, explaining the movie to me.

On the little screen there appeared an old man. Around him were a young woman wearing a long white dress and three children—a boy and two girls. The old man points to the trees inside Canada Park, which was planted with green grass, and where there were lots of swings and playgrounds for children.

The old man stopped walking among the trees and began explaining to his daughter and grandchildren. He was not explaining to them, he was explaining to the camera, talking to the camera as though he were talking to a person. He bent down to the ground and began to draw with his finger on the green grass an outline of the house that was no longer there. He stopped a long time in front of the kitchen and talked about the washing machine he had bought just three months before the house was demolished. He stood up and led them to where the graveyard was. A field of green grass, and all the names erased.

That man was not the reason Emil left.

The reason he left was Gaza. There, in front of al-Shati' Refugee Camp, they rounded up all the males between the ages of fourteen and seventy. After standing for six hours beneath the burning August sun with hundreds of other men, the old man asked permission to go to the bathroom. Emil, who had been drafted into the army at age twenty, granted him permission. The man got out of line, and began walking in that horrible manner. He got down on his knees, put his hands on the ground, and started moving backward, afraid they would shoot him in the back.

Samia didn't ask me how they shot Nabeela.

When I went to Shatila, all Samia asked about was Nabeela and Nabeela's only daughter, but she never asked how she was killed.

I wanted her to ask. I had prepared myself for her questions, and I prepared my answers to questions such as, "How did they shoot? Where? Did they shoot her from behind? Or face to face?"

And Nabeela was.

1962: Good Shepherd Secondary School in Ashrafiyyeh. We were in seventh grade, and Nabeela Sulbaq was telling us about Palestine. She gave me a book by Nicholas al-Durr entitled *That Was How It Was Lost, and That Is How It Will Return*. All I remember about the book is its red cover, and Nabeela's excitement and pride when she told us the author was a friend of her father's and that he often came to their house to visit.

1988: I searched in Ashrafiyyeh, which is also called "Little Mountain," for Good Shepherd Secondary School, but I didn't find it. The highway had been built through Ashrafiyyeh, and all the street signs and landmarks had been changed. And, having left Ashrafiyyeh during the civil war, I no longer knew where anything was. I found military checkpoints and armed men with black beards. I got close to where the school had been. I was in front of it. My school had been turned into the main headquarters for the militias of the "Lebanese Forces."

1966: I visited Nabeela at her house in Ayn al-Rumani, in the suburbs of East Beirut. The occasion was our having passed the baccalaureate. That was the first and last time I went to her house, and there I met her youngest sister whose beautiful eyes enchanted me.

1976: The Phelangist militia entered the house in Ayn al-Rumani. Her father, mother and little sister with the beautiful eyes were there. They killed them all. The little girl's body was found hidden near the bed. She had been slaughtered with an ax.

1986: West Beirut, during the war of the camps when the Amal militias tried to take control of the Palestinian refugee camps in Beirut. Nabeela was riding in a taxi on her way home from work at UNICEF where she was responsible for the health and humanitarian aid program for the Palestinian camps. Her house was in the Barbour district. They stopped the car—three armed men—and opened fire with their Kalashnikovs. When Nabeela got out of the car, she knew it was all over. She knew the three armed men wearing black face masks held her death in their hands. She stepped out of the car and began walking away. One of the men tried to ask her something. He had been standing beside her when she got out of the car. She didn't respond, or turn her head. She saw the taxi speed away with its terrified passengers. She walked, and so they fired. Maybe she heard the first shot; then her body began to be ripped apart as it was strewn on the sidewalk in splotches of water and blood. The armed men left the place casually, as if they had done nothing, and Nabeela was left there, tossed into the street, near Hamada's Barbecue restaurant.

I told Samia about the funeral at Saints Peter and Paul Church in Hamra. I told her how no one talked to anyone, and how two armed men showed up who looked like the killers. They stood in front of the church door with sleepy, empty eyes. The church pews wailed in silence as we sat looking at one another's long faces, not saying anything. The priest stood before the altar and gave a sermon on love. He stopped talking as tears began to roll down over his white beard. Then he said to her—he said to us—that he didn't want to preach to us, but to the victim. He didn't use the word *martyr*. He said "the victim." And he continued, "I say to you that they killed you because you are Palestinian," and he burst into tears.

I said to Samia, "We didn't know you were all here in the camp. You couldn't have funeral processions anymore because you ran out of space, and had to do away with graves."

That day I understood Um Ahmad. She took me by the arm to the mass graveyard inside the camp. It had been created for the victims of the 1982 massacre of Sabra and Shatila. I understood how happy she was when she said they succeeded in building the graveyard and fencing it in. She showed me those strange flowers growing over the roof of the mass graveyard.   ◆

What am I telling?

The truth is I don't know how. But we didn't go to Lucolus Restaurant; I hadn't heard of that restaurant yet, where all the rich people of Beirut went, and whose prices were sky high. Mary and I got to the bottom floor of the building, where we saw a half-destroyed sign with the name of the restaurant on it. We decided we would come back in a week, with food and drinks, so we could get drunk on the balcony of destruction. But we didn't go back. It's always like that. We decide and then we don't go. Then, after time passes, events get mixed up in my mind, and I remember things that didn't happen as if they really did.

But Nabeela did happen.

And Ali Abu Tawq.

And Faysal Ahmad Salem.

And the white Circassian.

As for Jurji the monk, he is a story.

With Jurji the monk the problem becomes clear.

His story, the way I told it to Mary, is incomplete. It's a collection of hypotheses, none of which is certain. What are we supposed to do when we are faced with this kind of situation? Do we forget the story? Or try to tell it in the most hypothetical terms?

In the past, stories of this kind were left in the hands of time. And so time would revise them and reshape them into myths of a sort, or folk stories at the very least. In the myth, the individual and collective components of the sub-conscious meld together; whereas in the folk story, these components become symbols that speak to the subcon-scious, and over time, they become children's stories.

Yet now we are living in the age of writing. That is, when we record the event at the very moment it occurs, we cancel its mythical potential. This is why Latin American writers resorted to the oral past in order to shape the myths of modern times. The Italian writer Umberto Eco, on the other hand, offered another suggestion—to turn ancient texts into hypothetical ones, and incorporate the written text into the modern myth. And Eco's supposition, despite its aesthetic appeal, remains merely a rational supposition. It does not offer a literary solution to the question of the story—myth.

With Jurji the monk, the problem is different.

We are faced with a short news item in a newspaper, the text of which does not say a whole lot. It says only that the man was shot to death. At the same time we are faced with a story told by an old woman from Miyyeh Miyyeh Refugee Camp. So which do we choose?

I wavered over the matter a lot. Certainly, Jurji the monk did not kidnap Jews on Good Friday, because kidnapping a Jew, in the 1940s, in Jerusalem, was logistically impossible. Yet the belief that he had was what made his story remain in popular memory—that is, the very vitality of the Lebanese monk's story is connected to an act he did not commit. In fact, he owes his entire existence as a story to the popular imagination. And therefore, cutting this event out of the story in order not to be accused of antisemitism by Mr. Emil Azayev will seem unfair in regard to the story, whereas it is necessary for the sake of truth. Do I cut out the very reason the story still exists? Or do I cut out the truth? Or do I cut out the story completely, and give up trying to write it . . . or write it incomplete?

And so, what?

I don't know. But what I have learned from my encounters with many people native to Jerusalem has enabled me to paint this picture of the monk. After fleeing from Saint Saba Monastery, Jurji the monk became the leader of a gang. He got some young men together and formed the Galilee gang that robbed from smugglers and distributed the loot to the poor in the Galilee and South Lebanon. "The Monk's Gang," as it was called, became everyone's greatest fear, to the extent that one of the leading smugglers, Ahmad al-Khawaja, made a deal with the monk that he would pay the monk and his gang protection money on each convoy. The monk and his group carried weapons, but they never used them, and Jurji the monk, in his black monk's robe and with his British rifle, saw himself in the image of Jesus Christ, holding His whip to expel the money-changers from the Temple.

The rifle was Christ's whip. That's what the monk believed, and that was why he never fired it except into the air.

Things went on that way for a few years, until the gang was ambushed by one of the "Jewish Kobbaniyyahs" as the Jewish settlements in the Galilee area were called at that time. The gang, carrying their weapons, was on the way to the outskirts of Nazareth when they were fired upon. Four of the six members were killed. No one was spared except the monk and a Jordanian man from Salt called Issa. The monk and Issa fled into the woods and hid for three days. On the fourth day Issa returned to Salt, and the monk went to Jerusalem where he rented a room in the Christian Quarter.

On Holy Thursday, the monk carried a huge cross and walked through the streets of Jerusalem shouting that he was carrying the cross of the Arabs. He reached the Jewish Quarter of the city, and there they stoned him.

Three days after that the monk was killed, and it was said that he was crazy, and he was this, and he was that . . .

The popular imagination was what added things on, and I am cutting things out, and that is not fair. That is why I say the monk was, just as he was in the story the woman in Miyyeh Miyyeh camp told me.

I don't remember if I told Emil Azayev any of this. I was busy working on a love story about a love that gets dizzy in the end. Love is like that; it gets dizzy before it ends. It gives the impression it is beginning, when it has already begun to vanish within the folds of the memory. What kind of memory is this that makes us believe that love has reached its peak just when it has already begun to slip toward its end which resembles memories.

But the story could take another form.

I went to Shatila. It was Monday, March 14, 1987. It was the first day the siege had been lifted from the camp after three long years. We reached the Syrian army check point that had been set up between the camp and the Amal fighters. After lots of questions and searches and so on, they allowed us to go inside.

I was going to visit Ali's grave.   ◆

Ali Abu Tawq was my friend. We spent the civil war years together, in the trenches and the cold and the death, beneath the rain of the bombs. Then we went separate ways. Ali became a freedom fighter in the Jarmaq Platoon, and I became what I am. After the Israeli invasion of Lebanon in 1982, Ali left on the Greek ships that carried the freedom fighters to their new exile. In 1984, after the February 6 uprising, and the withdrawal of the U.S. Marines, Ali returned to Beirut, with his short beard and his cane and ended up as the military commander for Shatila. He came back to live under the siege—three years of siege and destruction, and the camp became more and more crowded with its demolished houses until it became something like a handful of houses, the one holding up the debris of the other.

And Ali died.

I heard the news on the radio.

On the morning of March 14, 1987, the first day after the siege was lifted, I went there. I knew that Ali loved a woman named Samia (of course, that's not her real name. I change women's names when I see they are in love because I think love changes everything about a woman, even her name.) I entered the camp, and I asked about the Fatah office. The roads in the camp got narrower and narrower; then they turned into heaps. The road disappeared. The heaps were the road, and the vile water covered the ground with that smell of death that seeps into your joints. The horizon collapsed onto the destroyed houses, entering into the windows. There was no horizon. In Shatila, the sky vanished inside the rubble, and the water turned into puddles inside the holes in the walls that had fallen to the ground.

I was walking along, holding onto the walls, slipping and walking. I went into an alley, the only alley that still existed amidst the destruction, and I asked about her. They led me to the Fatah office. I went up the three cement steps and went into a dimly lit room. I saw young men and women in army clothes sitting on the low couches and chairs as though they were relaxing after long, nervous hours of work. Then a woman came with coffee. The steam and the aroma rose into the air. Fresh coffee opens up your heart. I held the small coffee cup with both hands. The March cold turned the steam from the coffee into white circles that rose up and vanished into the ceiling. I held the cup and drank.

And she entered.

She approached me, hugged me, and kissed me on each cheek. Her hair was black and wet and dangling over her shoulders. She was wearing a white wool jacket, and the smell of perfumed soap enveloped her.

"You are Faysal," she said.

I don't know why she called me Faysal, for she knew my name.

She took me by the hand, and we went out. I didn't ask where we were going, for I was taken by the scent of Samia having just come out of the shower, smelling of perfumed soap, the elegance of the destruction hovering around her like halos.

She took me by the hand on a journey through the alleyways.

She asked me if I wanted to visit his grave.

We walked toward the grave. It wasn't a grave. We stopped in front of the window of the demolished mosque.

"They're all here," she said, pointing to the floor of the mosque. "All of them—Ali, and Faysal, and everyone."

The floor of the mosque was covered with wild flowers and weeds, and Samia was beside me, and something resembling sadness. She held my hand. I turned toward her. I wanted to tell her I loved her. I turned and hugged her. My head fell onto her shoulder, and I smelled the white woolen jacket. It was the scent of a lamb out in the sun.

"This is the mosque," she said. "We've turned it into a graveyard."

"Where are the tombstones?" I asked.

"No tombstones," she said. "They're all here. Ali, and Faysal, and you and me. Didn't you come to visit them?"

I stood in front of the mosque that had been turned into a graveyard, in front of the graveyard that doesn't look like the mosque, and her hand was in mine. Her hand felt so tender it nearly slipped away. I turned to her. Her eyes were wide open, with no tears.

She pulled me by the hand to continue our tour. I don't know how we came face to face again. I hugged her close to my chest, and I knew I couldn't reveal my love to her.

> Joseph,
> When he saw that the sun had hidden its rays,
> And the veil of the Temple was rent at the death of the Savior,
> Approaching Pilate, pleading with him, crying out and saying:
> Give me this Stranger,
> Who from his youth has wandered like a stranger,
> Give me this Stranger,
> Whom his kinsmen killed in hatred like a stranger,
> Give me this Stranger,
> At whom I wonder, beholding him as a Guest of death,
> Give me this Stranger,
> Whom the Jews in envy estranged from the world,
> Give me this Stranger,
> That I may bury him in a tomb,
> Give me this Stranger,
> Who being a Stranger,
> Hath no place whereon to lay his head,
> Give me this Stranger,

To whom his Mother, beholding him dead,
Cried, My son and my God,
Give me this Stranger,

In these words the honourable Joseph pleaded with Pilate,
Took the Saviour's body,
And with fear wrapped it in linen and balm,
And placed it in a tomb.

After the fall of the camp, Samia moved to Sidon, and I never saw her again.

I am the one who saw,

I bear witness, and I say, and I shout,

I am the one standing on the shore of the Dead Sea, where the mirrors and the copper faces are, where the earth is separated from the earth.

I said to Mary that I want to tell her. I told her about Samia, who left, and about this life we wear like a shroud.

Is she Mary? The one sitting at the edge of the Jordan Valley, waiting for the stranger who is killed by the stranger? Or is she the story?

Is this land whose name is Palestine merely a story that bewitches us with its secrets and its charms?

And why is it when we listen to this story we don't fall asleep . . . we die?